THE DOOMSDAY TRAIL

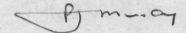

Also by Peter J Murray

MoKee Joe
IS COMING

MoKee Joe
RECHARGED

Bonebreaker

Coming soon:

Dawn Demons

MOKEE JOE

THE DOOMSDAY TRAIL

PETER J MURRAY

I dedicate this book to the growing army of Mokee Joe fans.
Their continued support and enthusiasm
has provided the inspiration for this book.

Copyright © 2005 Peter Murray
Illustrations © 2005 Simon Murray

First published in Great Britain in 2005
by Hodder Children's Books
This edition published by Mokee Joe Promotions in 2007

3 5 7 9 10 8 6 4

A Catalogue record for this book is available from the British Library

ISBN-10: 0 955 34153 1
ISBN-13: 978 0 955 34153 3

Typeset in Garamond by Avon DataSet Ltd,
Bidford-on-Avon, Warwickshire

Printed in the UK by CPI Bookmarque, Croydon, CR0 4TD

The paper and board used in this paperback by Mokee Joe Promotions
are natural recyclable products made from wood grown in sustainable forests.
The manufacturing processes conform to the environmental regulations
of the country of origin.

Mokee Joe Promotions
Riversdale
8 Rivock Avenue
Steeton
BD20 6SA
tel 01535 656015

www.peterjmurray.co.uk

Prologue

The sea-witch stood alone on the edge of the shore staring out towards the starlit horizon. She knew that the time had almost arrived.

Her matted hair, like tangled seaweed, blew back in the stiffening onshore breeze, her bedraggled gown rippled like the gentle waves before her. Hour after hour she stood there, still as a statue, staring out to sea – *and then she saw it*.

At first, a shining light like all the other countless stars, but this light was moving – like a distant plane. And with every passing second, the light grew bigger and brighter. As it moved away from the horizon it gave the impression that it was rising, but in reality it was dropping like a stone, rapidly descending from the heavens.

The silent observer, still rooted to the spot, threw her head back and watched the fireball move ever closer. A faint drone quickly turned into a thunderous roar as a blinding light filled her field of vision, forcing her to stagger backwards and shield her eyes.

As the fireball struck the sea, she put her hands to her ears. But there was no deafening bang; instead a powerful thud followed by a great flash of light and then all went quiet.

The sea-witch moved to the edge of the shore, took a last look out to sea, and scanned the beach to see if any others had witnessed what she had seen. But there was no one.

She turned and made her way back to the lonely beach hut, stepped inside and warmed herself in front of an ancient woodburning stove. She glanced up at the old clock as it chimed a solitary chime – it was 4.15 am. She pushed another piece of driftwood into the stove, sat back in her rocking chair and stared towards the door.

Before long, she knew she would have visitors.

1

Confusion

The gentle waves that Hudson had been so pleasantly dreaming about suddenly seemed real. It was as if he could actually hear them lapping against the shore. Beneath him, the ground felt hard and there was a strong smell of seaweed.

As the pain in his right leg began to throb more intensely, his dream slowly turned into a restless nightmare – until he awoke.

At least he thought he was awake.

He opened his eyes and found himself staring up at a starlit sky. But he could still hear the waves and smell the sea.

Finally his brain registered – *this was reality!*

But he had absolutely no idea where he was or what was happening. And that's when the panic set in.

Meanwhile, Molly lay by his side in the darkness. She was still dreaming . . . of her parents . . . of her father with his curly, black hair and thick moustache . . . of her mother – always smiling, always asking about Hudson and what he was up to . . . of Sampson, her golden Labrador – the best dog in the world – how she missed him . . .

'*Molly – wake up!*'

Molly jolted back to wakefulness. She stared up at Hudson with wide eyes. 'What's happened? Where on Earth are we?'

Hudson clutched at his leg as he answered. 'That's just the point. We shouldn't be on Earth, but I think we are. Look!'

He pointed upwards and Molly followed his gaze. Despite the approaching dawn, the moon still shone in the darkened sky, its craters forming the familiar face of the 'man in the moon'.

'That's *our* moon,' Molly said, her voice shaking as she tried to stand up. 'Where are we and what's this we're lying in . . . and what are all these strings and cloth . . . and why are you holding your leg? *Hudson . . . what's going on?*'

Hudson wished he knew!

His mind reeled with recent events – at least he thought they were recent.

It seemed only hours ago that they had been standing amongst the huddled groups of scientists and officials by the launch site of the homebound spaceship. He remembered Molly's dumbfounded expression as GA had explained to her that should she choose to accompany them back to Hudson's home planet, Alcatron 3, it would be possible for her to make the subsequent journey home along a time loop, so that a whole year away would only seem like a day to anyone on

Earth. Molly had been thrilled at the prospect and had agreed enthusiastically – her parents wouldn't be too angry with her for one day's unannounced absence. And then Hudson recalled his elation as he'd stood by Molly's side gazing out from inside the ship, the stars growing bigger, the ground lights below growing smaller as they'd accelerated away into the depths of space . . .

'Hudson! Stop dreaming!' Molly said sharply, bringing him back to his senses.

'Sorry!' He strained his eyes and looked around, his brain trying desperately to work out exactly where they were and what had gone wrong.

It seemed to him that they had been washed up on a beach and were lying in some sort of life raft – a heavy rubber dinghy – the 'strings and cloth' as Molly had put it, was most likely some sort of parachute. His leg throbbed again and he looked down at the blackened hole burnt in the silver material just above his right knee. His memory began to clear a little.

'The ship . . . it crashed into the sea. I remember being ejected in an escape vessel and then . . . nothing . . . it all went black. We've obviously been washed up . . . and I think something hot caught my leg. I've got a burn . . . look.'

Molly crawled across the floor of the dinghy and examined Hudson's leg.

'That looks nasty. It'll need seeing to. Let's get out of this thing and try to see where we are. Can you manage?'

Hudson was already half over the side as he replied. 'Yes, it hurts like mad, but I can still walk. Come on, let's have a look around.'

A few seconds later they were both standing on firm, moist sand, looking down a deserted strip of beach, sand dunes silhouetted against the night sky on one side, a calm sea on the other. There was nothing else.

The two lonely figures suddenly turned and faced one another as the inevitable questions sprang into their minds.

'Where's GA?' Hudson asked.

Molly looked back at him with a shocked expression on her face. 'And what about Mokee Joe?'

'With a bit of luck, he'll be in a million pieces at the bottom of the sea,' Hudson muttered, with more than a hint of anger in his voice.

Molly grabbed Hudson's wrist and shook it anxiously. 'And what about GA? You don't suppose . . .'

'I don't know and I don't even want to think about that possibility. Come on . . . let's wander down the beach and see what we can find. But be on your guard. Anything could happen.'

Molly looked down at the silver spacesuit she was wearing. Her eyes filled with wonder. 'With you around, Hudson, you're absolutely right. Anything *could* happen!'

Hudson was the first to see the black, shadowy shape in the distance. 'Molly, look! There in front!'

As they edged forward, it became obvious that the object was another escape vessel. Just like their own, it lay motionless, washed up on the sand, the strings and material of the parachute sprawled beside it.

'You stay here, Moll. I'll go and take a look.'

Thinking about the *two* spaceship passengers still

unaccounted for, Molly peered nervously around. 'OK, but be careful. I'll watch your back and yell out if I see anything.'

'Fine . . . I'll only be a minute . . . here goes.' Hudson crouched low and started towards the dinghy.

He crept slowly across the sand, his heart beating faster with every step. Somehow he sensed that the dinghy wasn't empty. He tensed his muscles and completely forgot about his injured leg.

'OK – let's take a look,' Hudson whispered to himself.

He crawled the final few metres on his hands and knees and peered over the edge of the dinghy. His eyes bulged wide as he saw its occupant, eyes as big as his own staring back.

'MOLLY! GET YOURSELF OVER HERE,' Hudson shouted. The deep gash in the front left lobe of his uncle's enlarged head glistened in the moonlight. 'IT'S GA – AND I THINK HE'S BADLY HURT.'

'You're exactly right, Tor-3-ergon,' Guardian Angel croaked. 'Time is of the essence. I do not have long to remain in my physical existence.'

Molly crept up and crouched by Hudson's side. She peered over the rim of the escape vessel and stared with horror-filled eyes at GA's face. 'What does he mean, Hudson?'

'That he's dying,' Hudson replied in a trembling voice.

'Earthly terms, as usual,' GA whispered, with a smile. 'There is nothing to fear for me. I am simply moving on to a higher plane. It is you and Molly that I fear for. The battle is far from over.'

'So is Mokee Joe still alive?' Hudson asked, climbing into the dinghy and kneeling by his uncle.

GA turned his head to look up at him. Hudson noted that his uncle's eyes looked huge and clear in the moonlight. 'He is very much alive and his mission to destroy you is more resolved than ever.'

Molly looked nervously over her shoulder towards the shadowy sand dunes. 'Is he close?' she whispered into the dinghy.

Without taking his eyes off Hudson, GA answered Molly's question: 'No. You have some time. He is out on the water – floating in a third escape vessel. He will take his time in coming ashore. He has a fear of salt water – it is corrosive and damaging to his physical make-up.'

'What happened to the spaceship?' Hudson asked.

GA took a deep breath and spoke in solemn tones: 'As we were passing out of the solar system and about to enter the hyper-speed phase, the ship encountered a large asteroid composed entirely of magnetic ore. It nudged the ship, and its magnetic field induced a massive surge of energy into Mokee Joe. He escaped his metal strapping and took the controls. He tried desperately to redirect the craft back to Earth – to make it crash. His mission would have been completed.'

'His mission to kill Hudson,' Molly stated quietly, her voice quaking.

'And what about him?' Hudson asked. 'Would he have destroyed himself?'

GA continued, his voice growing weaker by the second: 'No . . . his instinct for self-preservation is strong. He intended to eject at the last moment, land on Earth and continue his reign of terror.'

'So what went wrong?'

'Even during sleep suspension my brain is in contact with the ship's automatic pilot. As events unfolded and our course fluctuated, I was alerted. I crept out of my sleep capsule and hid behind the creature. I read his every thought and then tried in vain to wrestle the controls from him, but alas, he struck me a savage blow to my head and left me for dead. I managed to crawl away and recover a little. The ship, already damaged in its encounter with the asteroid, was clearly out of Mokee Joe's control. My only hope was to get to the ejection vessels before it plummeted to its fate. I was able to operate the escape pods, one for the two of you and one for myself, and for a moment I thought only the ship and the creature would be destroyed and all our problems would be solved.'

'But I suppose Mokee Joe managed to escape too,' Hudson joined in.

GA's voice faltered further. 'Yes, I'm afraid so. As we three were launched towards the stars, I saw the Mokee Man eject just before the spaceship struck the sea.' GA hesitated; his voice began to break up. 'Tor-3-ergon . . . I have little time left : . .'

Suddenly realising that his one true relative and strongest ally was about to die, Hudson went very quiet. Tears began to form in the corners of his eyes.

'Don't be upset,' GA whispered, 'your powers are almost fully developed and you will prove a formidable adversary in the continuing battle against Mokee Joe. You are strong in mind and body and a credit to your race. Your mother would have been proud of you.'

Hudson noted that GA didn't mention his father – the person responsible for all their problems – the creator of Mokee Joe, his terminator.

GA reached out and took hold of Hudson's hand. 'Tor-3-ergon, listen carefully . . . you must find the sea-witch. She will see you safely on your way . . .'

'Way . . . where . . . sea-witch . . .' Hudson stammered. His uncle's hand felt cold and clammy and he sensed that GA was almost through.

'You must return to Danvers Green . . . lead your enemy there . . . your destiny awaits you among the old marshes . . . the sea-witch will help you . . .'

Hudson squeezed his uncle's hand tight. 'But, but . . .'

'No more time,' GA sighed, closing his eyes. 'I must leave you and Molly now. Stay close to each other. You make a formidable team.'

'GA . . . please don't leave us,' Molly cried. 'I'm sure we can save you. Your injuries . . .'

'It is more than injuries,' GA interrupted softly. 'My time in this dimension is through. I am tired and ready to move on.'

Tears rolled down Hudson's cheeks as he felt GA's hand loosen its grip. His bottom lip began to tremble as he watched a faint smile break out on his uncle's craggy face and then . . . GA spoke no more.

For a few seconds, that seemed to stretch to eternity, a silent stillness descended over everything and then Hudson and Molly lurched backwards and gasped in unison as an intense point of light emitted from GA's head. It shot into the air like a miniature shooting star and hovered high above them. The two friends climbed out of the dinghy and stood side by side. They clung to each other and watched in awe as the bright light rose higher towards the heavens. And then a great gust of wind blew from nowhere and they shielded their eyes from the stinging clouds of sand.

Then the strange light disappeared and all went quiet again – just the sound of gently lapping waves.

Hudson went numb with shock, until he felt Molly tugging at his arm. 'Come on, let's find somewhere to sit and we'll wait until it gets fully light. We can't do much until then.'

Hudson nodded and the two of them crept over towards the foot of a steep sand dune. They sat in the shadows, snuggled up against each other, desperately trying to keep warm. Neither spoke. Instead, they dozed gently and both wondered if it was all a dream, and perhaps that they were still sleeping in the spaceship gliding silently through space. It was only when the bright dawn sun rose on the distant horizon and roused them to wakefulness that they realised this was no dream.

2

STRIKER

Hudson's eyes blinked in the strong morning light. Molly was standing across from him on the firm sand. She had her hands on her hips and appeared to be looking out to sea. A flock of seagulls wheeled above her head; the sound of their screeching drifting away on the strengthening offshore breeze.

'Hey, Hudson! Come and take a look.'

Hudson rubbed his eyes and glanced at his leg. The pain had got worse. He struggled to his feet and limped over to join Molly. On the way he instinctively glanced out to sea – to where she was looking. Above the growing waves the sky was clear and blue, but far out on the horizon a thin ribbon of dark cloud filled the gap between the sea and the clear sky.

'What do you make of it, Hudson?'

'It looks like some sort of approaching storm.'

'Or maybe some sort of approaching Mokee Joe,' Molly muttered, almost to herself. 'I'm sure I can see streaks of blue lightning striking out there, below that line of black cloud.'

'Yes, he's out there somewhere and we need to move fast. But first, we need to find out where *we* are and then we can start looking for this sea-witch.'

Molly shivered and stroked her chin with an index finger. 'Yes, I wonder who she is? It's a pity Ash isn't here . . . he might have come up with something.'

Hudson went quiet. He thought about their friend and wondered where he might be and what he was up to . . . probably still in bed!

He snapped himself back to the present. 'Look . . . I think we should cover our tracks. Let's hide GA's body and the two escape vessels and then we ought to move on.'

'How about your leg? I can see you're still in pain.'

'Don't worry. I'll get it looked at later. Come on, we've got to get away from here.'

For the next hour Hudson and Molly struggled to fold up the parachute material and drag the escape vessels over to the dunes. They made the job easier by puncturing the dinghies and tearing up the parachute material with the aid of some sharp razor shells washed up on the shoreline.

Hudson scraped a shallow hole in the sand with his bare hands and with Molly's help they slid GA's body into it. It broke Hudson's heart to bury GA, but at the same time it made him feel better. The shallow grave seemed to add an air of dignity to the farewell of his uncle.

By the time they had cleared up, Hudson could hardly walk. He knew he needed to take immediate action. As the two friends sat exhausted, side-by-side in the shelter of the dunes, Hudson raised his knee and tore the material of his spacesuit away from the wound to reveal blackened, shrivelled flesh.

Molly grimaced. 'That looks really bad, Hudson. What are you going to do?'

He took a strip of parachute material he'd stored earlier in his pocket and passed it to her. 'Could you take this over to the sea and soak it?'

Without question, Molly did as she was asked. She returned a few seconds later and watched as Hudson tied the strip soaked in seawater tightly around the wound. He winced as the brine soaked into the infected tissue, and then he limped into the middle of the beach.

Molly sat and shivered and clutched her knees close to her chest. She watched as Hudson scanned around taking in the surroundings.

'Apart from the gulls, there's no sign of life, Moll,' Hudson shouted across to her.

'Hudson . . . what's that bobbing in the sea?' she shouted back.

He turned his head, looked back and saw a yellow plastic ball rising and falling amongst the waves.

'Just a ball! It's coming in.'

Molly joined him and they both stared out to sea watching the ball come closer with every breaking wave. After a few minutes Hudson reached in and plucked it from the water. For a split second, the ball made him feel like a normal child again – back at the Browns' house in Tennyson Road – before the nightmare started . . .

Molly tapped him on the shoulder and jolted him back to his senses. 'Come on, Hudson. Remember – we need to get away from here.'

Hudson turned back to face the sand dunes. With hardly any effort, he threw the ball far into the distance so that it landed among the long grass bordering the top of the dunes.

As the ball disappeared from view, the sound of barking reached their ears.

'A dog!' Molly shrieked in surprise. 'Perhaps somebody's out taking it for a walk.'

Before Hudson had a chance to reply, the ball mysteriously reappeared above the top of the tall grass and then it floated in a very spooky way down the sandy slope, back towards them. Finally, a Jack Russell terrier shot out from the foot of the dunes carrying the plastic ball in its mouth. It dropped the ball on the firm sand and dribbled it with its nose towards the two friends.

'Wow – that dog's got real skill,' Molly giggled as the brown and white terrier controlled the ball perfectly and brought it to her feet. She kicked it away again. 'There he goes,' she shouted in delight as the dog tore after it at full speed and started dribbling it back. The little dog delivered the ball to her feet again and barked enthusiastically. Molly bent down, stroked it affectionately and reached for the metal tag hanging from its collar.

'Look, Hudson – there's a letter "S" stamped on its identity disc.'

'That dog's a brilliant footballer,' Hudson mused. 'Perhaps it stands for "Striker".'

'What a fab name,' Molly agreed. 'Who's a good boy then?' She tickled the dog's ear. 'Good boy, Striker! Good boy!'

The dog wagged his tail and then turned and walked away, all the time looking over his shoulder and barking determinedly.

'Hudson . . . I think Striker wants us to follow.'

But Hudson's mind was elsewhere. He'd been distracted and was staring out to sea. 'Moll, we really need to be on our way. *Look!*'

Molly turned and peered towards the horizon. The distant thin ribbon had broadened to a wide band of ominous black clouds. As they loomed ever nearer, the sea began to roar and the waves crashed in with much more force.

'There really is a storm brewing,' she said, her voice suddenly taking on a nervous edge. 'In fact . . . that is definitely blue lightning out there, isn't it?'

'Yes – and if you look really hard you'll see something else – something bobbing on the sea.' He pointed to a distant black object, appearing and disappearing among the waves, growing bigger with every second. He turned and looked at Molly's face and watched her expression change from childish curiosity to stark terror.

'It's him, isn't it? Mokee Joe! He's out there and heading this way?'

Before Hudson could reply, the dog was sitting at

their feet again, front paws up in the air and barking enthusiastically.

'Go, boy! Go! No more time for games,' Hudson shouted into the wind. 'Come on, Moll! Run!'

As the two friends set off running one way, the dog set off running in the opposite direction. And then the little animal turned and barked loudly at them.

Hudson and Molly stopped and looked at each other.

'It's only a hunch,' Hudson shouted above the wind, 'but "S" could . . .'

'. . . stand for sea-witch,' Molly finished.

The dog barked again from the distance.

'We've nothing to lose, let's follow him,' Hudson shouted.

As they turned and ran towards the terrier, Molly leading and Hudson limping behind, his leg began to throb again. He clenched his teeth, struggled on, and followed his companions away from the flat sand and up to the top of the dunes.

He still didn't have a clue where they were or where they were heading and absolutely no idea who the sea-witch might be or whether she really existed at all. The lightning was flashing around them and a thunderous roar rang through the sky as the rain arrived – things really couldn't get any worse – that is until Hudson took a last look over his shoulder.

The black object they had observed earlier was grinding up on to the beach. Though it was a long way off, it was easy to make out the dinghy with the tall frightening figure climbing out of it. Even through the storm it was possible to see the eerie blue glow.

Hudson swallowed hard as he watched the distant figure kick the dinghy savagely back into the sea. It turned, took several steps up the beach and then stood there, scanning around as if trying to get its bearings.

Finally, as it looked towards Hudson, it began to move forward taking great strides. Hudson wasn't sure whether it had seen him or not, but then it broke into a sinister, spider-like run and began charging in his direction.

3

The Sea-Witch

The ferocity of the storm eased slightly as the three fugitives ran along the track at the top of the sand dunes running parallel with the beach – Striker leading the way, Molly close behind and Hudson moving quickly, but still limping, at the back. He kept glancing over his shoulder, always expecting to see Mokee Joe hot on his heels, but thankfully, his enemy was nowhere in sight. Finally, much to Hudson's relief, Molly shouted over her shoulder, 'I can see caravans – Striker seems to be heading towards them.'

Hudson acknowledged her by raising a thumb. He knew he couldn't go on for much longer – he was growing weaker with every step.

As they neared the caravan park, Striker stopped and

turned to face them. He barked loudly and began jumping up and down – as if he knew something.

The caravans were in a field on their left. On their right, a wide strip of beach reached out to the sea from the bottom of the dunes. Much to their surprise, Striker headed off down towards the beach.

'Wait here, Hudson,' Molly ordered. 'I'll follow him and take a look.'

Hudson was only too glad to rest for a minute. Though the rain had slowed a little, he was soaked to the skin. He looked behind, back over the dunes. The sky was black, the storm just behind them, but at least there was still no sign of Mokee Joe.

'HUDSON! DOWN HERE! YOU'D BETTER COME AND TAKE A LOOK!'

Hudson grimaced and made his way down to the foot of the dunes. He heard Striker barking somewhere in the distance.

'What have you found?' he shouted, as he stepped on to the beach.

'Look – up there. It's got to be her place – the sea-witch.'

Hudson followed Molly's gaze and saw the wooden hut, almost hidden by tall sea grasses, nestled on a levelled-out area towards the bottom of the dunes. Striker stood close to a gate, wagging his tail. The two friends walked on towards it.

As they drew closer, Hudson saw that the small building was painted green, but much of the paint had long since cracked or disappeared. In fact, the entire hut looked in a state of poor repair. The roof had sagged and a piece of smoking pipe that seemed to act as a chimney stuck out from it at a precarious angle. But it was the sight of the 'garden' surrounding the old hut that provided the most interest.

'Blimey! What do you make of this, Hudson?'

Everywhere, were shells – thousands and thousands of them – arranged in the most spectacular way. Most of the simple smaller shells were laid out in attractive patterns whilst the larger and more intricate shells were built into three-dimensional structures like castles, seahorses and mermaids.

'Wow! I've never seen anything like it,' Hudson said, running a hand through his hair and gazing around.

Meanwhile, Molly had approached the gate and was busy looking up the path towards the door. 'Hudson . . . get this!'

He looked to where she was pointing and gasped with amazement.

The top half of the door had four panes of glass in it and each pane contained the image of a spooky face. In fact all the windows had faces in them, some spookier than others, but all seemed to be witch-like, with long hair made up from trailing strands of different types of seaweed. As the rain ran down the glass the faces seemed to move and change shape.

'Wow, this place is really weird . . .' Hudson said quietly.

'But it's got to be the right sort of place for someone known as the sea-witch, hasn't it?' Molly replied.

'Yes,' Hudson agreed, 'no doubt about it. Come on . . .'

The two of them cautiously followed Striker through the gate, up a path of rough wooden planking, and a moment later they were standing outside the weather-beaten door. Hudson took a deep breath and prepared to knock, but before he had the chance a voice sounded from inside and he jumped back in surprise: 'Don't stand outside in the rain . . . come in . . . I've been expecting you!'

Hudson pushed on the door – it creaked open allowing a warm glow to reach out and greet his cold, wet body.

As Hudson entered with Molly just behind his shoulder, Striker brushed past their legs and shot forward to greet the strange figure sitting in front of them. She sat in a wooden rocking chair by the side of some sort of stove – a black pipe coming out of the top of it and reaching up to the roof. Striker wagged his tail and panted enthusiastically. She reached down and stroked him.

'You two seem to know each other,' Hudson said.

'The dog and I are old friends. Close the door. Come and sit by me,' she replied in a quiet, throaty voice. 'We don't have much time. Is the dog looking after you? I hope so . . . he's as bright as a button and if he likes you he will stick by you like a limpet to a rock.'

Hudson and Molly were already staring around in wonder. It was the strangest room they had ever set foot in. The walls were decked with rough wooden shelves containing endless bottles and jars, their contents mostly liquids of varying shades of green; some having pieces of seaweed and shells in them. Bits of old fishing nets hung from the ceiling; some had fish skeletons inside – they looked sinister.

'We've named him Striker. You should see him control a ball . . .'

The old woman smiled and looked up at them. Her face was wrinkled and she had the appearance of someone very old. She beckoned them to come and sit on a well-worn rug by her feet. As they drew nearer, they saw that her hair was long and uncared for – greasy, matted, falling loosely over her hunched shoulders in shades of grey, black and green.

'So you're Hudson and Molly? You two have been having quite a time of it.'

'How does she know our names?' Molly whispered in Hudson's ear.

The woman seemed to hear her. 'I know more than most, dear. I'm a transcendent level 3.'

Hudson was really interested now. He sat quickly on the rug and Molly sat by his side, both of them captivated by the old woman's all-knowing tone of voice.

Hudson was about to ask what a transcendent level 3 was, but the woman spoke up again.

'It means that I can pick up thought waves, sometimes from a great distance. It depends on the power of the sender. Your uncle had great power. I read him easily.'

At the mention of GA, a mixture of excitement and sorrow welled up in Hudson's stomach. 'So GA spoke to you?' he asked, moving into a kneeling position and edging closer.

The woman leaned out of her chair and stirred two tin mugs on top of the stove. 'More than once. He contacted me before your ship crashed. He spoke to me after it had crashed – when he was out there on the waves. He told me many things and much of it to pass on to you. Your uncle was kind and caring and devoted to your well-being.'

Hudson stared again at the woman. She was dressed in some sort of black gown, and it was creased and covered in stains. It looked as if it had never been washed. As she placed her hands back on the arms of the chairs, he noticed that although they looked old – like her face – the nails were cared for, long, manicured and painted green. Hudson also noticed that Molly couldn't take her eyes off them.

'Now let's get that leg seen to,' the woman suddenly said, rising from her chair.

Hudson had momentarily forgotten about it. He glanced at Molly. 'Wow . . . she really does know everything,' he whispered.

'She's amazing,' Molly whispered back.

'Those pictures on the windows . . . the faces . . . who are they?' Hudson asked, unable to contain his curiosity.

'Old relatives,' the sea-witch answered. 'They all had the power, but only the last two generations and myself succeeded in reaching level 3.' She pointed to two particularly spooky portraits contained in the top two panels of the door.

And then she got up, walked over to the side of the room and lifted a jar from one of the shelves. Like most of the others, it seemed to contain a green liquid, but there were small white things floating about in it.

'Now, let's have that spacesuit off, young man,' the sea-witch suddenly ordered. 'And you, Molly – go through into my bed chamber.' She pointed to a door in the far corner of the room. 'You'll find some fresh clothes on the bed. Change into them.'

Molly raised her eyes and looked at Hudson with a bemused expression on her face. Hudson shrugged his shoulders.

The sea-witch returned to her chair with the jar in one hand and a piece of sponge in the other. 'Well . . . what are you waiting for?' she said impatiently, more towards Molly than Hudson. 'We've got very little time . . .'

Molly made her way across the cluttered room and disappeared through the door.

The old woman sat back in her chair, put the jar on top of the stove, and rocked back and forth a couple of times. Suddenly, she stopped rocking and went very silent. Hudson's heart filled with alarm as he saw the pupils in her eyes roll backwards. He gulped and swallowed hard as the sea-witch spoke again in a throaty, spooky voice: '*Hudson, listen to me. We really don't have much time. Mokee Joe is coming . . . I can feel his presence . . . he'll be here before we know it!*'

4

Powers & Potions

The sea-witch dabbed the strong-smelling potion on to Hudson's wound. It seeped deep into the infected tissue and stung like mad. But Hudson never flinched.

'You're a brave boy and that's no lie,' the old woman said with a sympathetic voice. 'This potion is the strongest disinfectant on Neptune's good Earth. It's a mixture of kelp, broad-leaved sea cress and brine.'

'What are those white things floating in it?' Hudson pointed at the jar.

'Mackerel brains – they're full of goodness.'

Hudson looked down at his wound. Already the blackened flesh was less shrivelled and the throbbing had stopped.

'You seem to be able to tune in to my enemy. I can usually

feel his presence too. I get headaches when he's around.'

The sea-witch stopped dabbing at his leg and began wrapping a length of bandage around it. 'The headaches are caused by his thought waves breaking in to your mind. In the great scheme of things, you and he are at least transcendents level 6.'

'What does transcendent level 6 mean?'

The woman beckoned Hudson to put on a navy blue tracksuit – it was hanging underneath a bag from a nail on the back of the door. 'It means that for generations my ancestors have slowly risen to spawn me with all my powers and potions, and you stand before me, a young thing, already twice as powerful. There's no justice!' she smiled. 'Now put that suit on.'

Hudson did as he was told and, just as he was pulling the trousers up around his knees, Molly appeared from the door in the corner already wearing hers. She giggled as Hudson quickly pulled the tracksuit bottoms up to his waist.

'What are these tracksuits for?' Molly asked the sea-witch.

'They're so you don't stand out on your journey. They're school uniforms.'

Hudson slipped into the tracksuit top and looked at the badge on the breast. It had a crest of two swords crossed over each other and the letters RSCS in the spaces between.

'Before you ask, Rye Sports Community School,' the woman said.

'These tracksuits are quite trendy,' Molly muttered, looking at the white stripes running down each of her arms. 'Is it really a school uniform?'

The sea-witch nodded impatiently and looked back to

Hudson. 'Now listen carefully. This is very important. And don't interrupt, there is so little time.'

Hudson and Molly knelt on the old rug and sipped hot tea from the tin mugs handed to them from off the top of the stove.

'You must lead the Mokee Joe devil back to Danvers Green.'

'I know . . . it was GA's last message to us,' Hudson said sadly.

'He is more determined than ever to get rid of you. If he is captured again he will destroy you, himself and everybody else.'

'How?' Hudson almost shouted in alarm.

The sea-witch went quiet for a moment. When she resumed, her voice had a slight tremble in it. 'Near here there is a nuclear power station. It produces unimaginable amounts of energy – enough to destroy all this land – should ever that power be used for the wrong purpose. Many people object to it being here.'

Hudson glanced across at Molly – to see if she understood.

She looked back, read his expression and spoke enthusiastically. 'They use radioactive materials – Uranium, Plutonium and suchlike. They're lethal. It's what atomic bombs are made of.'

Hudson nodded. He was impressed.

'Yes, young lady, you're right,' the sea-witch continued, 'and your spacecraft had a nuclear core. It produced the infinite amounts of energy needed to project it through hyperspace back to Alcatron 3.'

Hudson went very quiet and stared at the old woman. She seemed to know everything. His leg completely forgotten, he focused on her eyes and found he could read her mind. '*Triotose!* Mokee Joe has it with him.'

'Exactly right,' the sea-witch replied, sitting forward impressed at Hudson's thought-reading skills. 'He took it from the ship before he ejected.'

'What's Triotose?' Molly asked nervously.

'It's the most dangerous material in the universe, according to Hudson's uncle,' the sea-witch continued. 'There was just one hundred grams of it in your ship's nuclear core, but enough to blow up a large section of this planet in the wrong hands.'

'Like Mokee Joe's hands?' Hudson interrupted again.

The sea-witch nodded gravely. 'Exactly! But his body will need to be charged up to extreme levels before he can detonate the charge . . .'

'. . . and trigger a nuclear explosion!'

'My God!' Molly cried out, putting her hands either side of her head. 'So Mokee Joe is now a walking nuclear bomb!'

Hudson and the sea-witch looked across at Molly's terrified expression and then back to each other.

'And that is why he can't be caught,' the sea-witch said grimly. 'You have to stay one step ahead of him and lead him back to . . .'

'. . . Danvers Green,' Hudson finished for her again, the blood rushing from his face.

The sea-witch leaned forward and grabbed Hudson's wrists and looked him straight in the eyes. 'Yes . . . you can only succeed by leading the monster back to Danvers Green. This was your uncle's most important message for you. Do you understand?'

Hudson nodded.

'Now take this – there is everything you will need for your journey.' She passed Hudson the rucksack that had been hanging on the back of the door. 'And now you must go quickly.'

'But where to?' Molly asked in exasperation. 'We don't know where we are.'

'You are on the south-east coast of England in the county called Kent. From this place, you must follow the dunes further east for a good ten minutes until you come to a tarmac road. Follow the road on for another half-mile until you come to a row of coastguards' cottages and a stone tower. You will find my son waiting there in an old green van. He will take you to the capital.'

'*To London?*' Hudson and Molly shouted together.

'Yes. And from there head north and west. You will soon find your bearings and arrive back at Danvers Green. Contact no one . . . not even your parents . . . not until you are home.'

Hudson and Molly looked at each other without speaking. And then Molly spoke up, her voice almost trembling with fear and excitement. 'Our parents . . . do you know if they are OK?'

The old woman looked edgy and shifted her gaze back towards the old wood stove. She put on another piece of wood. 'Leave your parents to me. I will reassure them that you are on your way . . . now you must go.'

Hudson tried to look into the sea-witch's eyes, but she kept looking away. He sensed she was hiding something. He tried to read her mind, but she seemed to be blocking him out. He tied his shoes and started slipping the rucksack on to his back. 'Before we leave, can I ask one last question . . . how many transcendents are there?'

The sea-witch got up and put her hands on Hudson's shoulders. 'There are more than a few people who claim to be able to read minds. Most of these people are frauds, but a small number are true transcendents, like me. They vary in their power. There are reputedly a few mystics in the Eastern Countries who have reached level 5, but none ever as strong as you. Now you must go . . . time is fast running out. My son is waiting. He is simple of mind, but he is good-natured and will ask few questions. He is keen to help – so go to him now. His name is Malcolm.'

Striker, who during all this time had been curled up asleep by the stove, suddenly jumped up and slunk slowly towards the door. He lowered himself down on his belly and started growling, all the hairs on the back of his neck standing on end.

The sea-witch walked over to the window and peered through. Striker began barking frantically as she jumped back and turned to face them with a look of total despair on her face. For the first time, Hudson and Molly heard her voice shake uncontrollably as she spoke: '*By all the gods of the sea . . . I fear it may already be too late. We have an unwelcome visitor outside and I suspect that it is your dreaded enemy – Mokee Joe!*'

5

First Strike

'**OK** . . . everyone stand back. Keep well out of the way.'

'Hudson? What are you going to do?' Molly cried out.

The sea-witch picked up Striker, still barking savagely, and held him in her arms.

Hudson placed himself directly in front of the door. He stared towards the four glass panels, clenched his fists and waited, concentrating hard, listening for any movement.

'OK – HERE HE COMES!'

The old wooden door almost broke off its hinges and the glass panes shattered into a thousand fragments as Mokee Joe's seven-foot frame smashed its way into the doorway.

The massive boots, covered in wet sand, remained rooted to the spot as the living nightmare stood there, water dripping from the frayed sleeves of the familiar grubby coat. The old felt hat, more crumpled than ever, spewed a mass of greasy wet hair around the terrifying face as it glared at Hudson.

Hudson braced himself for the strike. His brain went into overdrive, anticipating Mokee Joe's line of attack and preparing a countermove calculated to precision.

As the demon rushed at him, he grabbed Mokee Joe's grubby coat by the lapels, swung him round one hundred and eighty degrees and hurled him back under his own momentum on top of the red-hot stove.

Such was the force of the impact that the old metal chimney broke away and the stove toppled on to its side. Mokee Joe lay sprawled back across it – burning logs spilling out on to the floor.

'QUICK – GO!' the sea-witch yelled as Striker jumped down from her arms and hared off outside.

Hudson and Molly followed. At the same time a high-pitched electronic scream rang through the air as Mokee Joe leapt to his feet, his clothes hissing and crackling as they caught fire. Hudson turned back and watched open-mouthed as the monster clawed at his coat, desperately trying to smother the flames; but every time he succeeded, the sea-witch threw some colourless liquid on to him and the flames roared up again.

'That woman . . . she's so brave,' Hudson yelled to Molly as they sprinted up the sandy slope and made off into the distance, his leg already feeling much stronger.

On and on they went, along the tops of the dunes. Finally, Hudson stopped and looked back, checking that Mokee Joe wasn't directly on their tail. But all he could see was a great tower of billowing black smoke rising up into the clearing blue sky.

His heart skipped a beat as he realised what had happened.

Molly walked back and saw the alarm on his face. 'What's up, Hudson? What's wrong?'

Hudson stared at the smoke. Thicker and thicker, blacker and blacker, the pall rose up above the distant dunes. His heart felt heavy and he swallowed hard. 'The sea-witch . . . her hut . . . that amazing place . . . it's burning to the ground!'

The sea-witch had underestimated the time for the first part of their onward journey. It was a good twenty minutes before they reached the narrow tarmac road and another ten minutes before the neat row of coastguards' cottages appeared. But at least the van was there, bright green and about as ancient as the old brick tower that stood by its side.

'Blimey, Hudson! It's a rust bucket!' Molly exclaimed as they ran up behind it.

Striker barked in agreement.

'I don't care as long as it goes,' Hudson replied. 'I hope the driver's inside.'

He was. The driver's door opened and a big, round man got out. He looked to be in his late twenties, but as he smiled, Hudson noted a childlike innocence in his expression.

'Hello. My name's Malcolm. Mum says I'm to take you up to London with me.'

He was wearing a pair of baggy, brown cord trousers and a big checked shirt with the sleeves rolled up. As he introduced himself he brushed a long fringe of auburn hair from the top of his plump, red face.

'That's right,' Hudson replied. 'I'm Hudson and this is Molly. Oh, and the dog's called Striker.'

'My mum calls him Smarty, 'cause 'e's clever. But you can call him Striker if you like,' Malcolm said in a simple sort of way. 'Are we taking him with us?'

'If that's OK,' Hudson answered. He'd taken a liking to Striker and sensed that the animal would prove to be a useful ally.

'Makes no difference to me. I'll let 'im in.'

Hudson and Molly went round to the passenger door and climbed in on to the long front seat. Malcolm let Striker into the back. Hudson looked over his shoulder and watched as the dog curled up by the side of some cardboard boxes stacked on the floor of the van.

The driver climbed in beside them and saw Hudson staring at his cargo. 'They're some of Mum's potions. I'm taking them up to the Government Research Hospital. I go up at least once a week. There's a man up there who buys them. His name's Derek. I think he does some kind of tests and things on them . . . nobody understands how they work, see.'

Hudson looked at Molly. Some of the things that Malcolm said sounded strange. But then his mother was very strange. And then Hudson thought about his leg. The pain had almost gone. It was healing fast, like the sea-witch said it would. 'Your mum's a clever woman,' Hudson said, nodding his approval.

Malcolm placed the keys in the ignition. 'Most people think Mum's weird. They won't go anywhere near . . . only to throw things and cause trouble. That's why she sells her sea potions by mail order. She makes 'em and I deliver 'em. It makes us both a bit of money and keeps us going.'

Hudson went quiet. He wondered whether Malcolm's mother had survived Mokee Joe's attack, but he said nothing. Meanwhile, Molly was busy looking over her shoulder and trying to peer through the small windows in the very back of the van. She'd watched a man and a woman jog past a few minutes earlier and thought she'd heard some shouting from behind.

'Hudson. I really think we ought to be on our way,' she said with concern in her voice. As she spoke, Striker jumped to his feet and sniffed the air. Malcolm turned the keys, but the engine didn't start.

Hudson looked behind and froze as he saw the tall, gangly figure in the distance. The driver turned the keys again and the engine spluttered into life.

Now Hudson and Molly both strained to see through the tiny rear windows as the familiar, terrifying figure loomed closer. 'Malcolm . . . is it OK if we get a move on?' Hudson asked, trying not to show too much panic in his voice.

'Going now,' the driver said, as the old van chugged slowly away. 'We'll take our time though . . . no hurry!'

Hudson looked at the speedometer. The needle flickered and climbed precariously to fifteen miles per hour. He looked through the cracked wing mirror and estimated that Mokee Joe was approaching at a speed of at least twenty miles per hour.

'Can we go any faster, Malcolm?' Hudson asked politely.

'We really do need to get a move on. You see, there's a bad man chasing after us.'

'Mum says I mustn't ever go too fast,' Malcolm replied in his childlike way. 'In any case, I'm not afraid of anyone.' He looked in the offside wing mirror and jerked his head in surprise when he saw the sinister figure closing from behind.

Again, Hudson watched the speedometer. It rose slowly up to twenty-five miles per hour, the van and everything in it beginning to rattle.

'Hudson, he's catching up with us,' Molly shrieked as Striker began to bark.

Without warning, a fierce bolt of electrical charge struck the van and the air inside crackled. Everyone's hair literally stood on end, Hudson's more than anyone's.

'What's happening?' Malcolm quivered. 'Was that the bad man?'

'Yes, Malcolm,' Hudson answered, his eyes firmly fixed on the back window. 'We need to go faster or the bad man will catch us.'

Molly gripped Hudson's arm. 'Hudson, he'll kill us all. He seems more determined – just like GA said. Look . . . he's aiming his fingers again . . .'

'We might just get away with it, Moll. The van's sitting on rubber tyres. They're protecting us . . . we just need to go faster.'

The air glowed blue and crackled as another surge of electricity hit the van. Hudson flattened his hair down and cursed under his breath. They'd now reached a speed of just over thirty miles per hour, but their pursuer was still closing in. Hudson and Molly could only watch in horror, as the dreaded vision of Mokee Joe became clearer. Now they could see the burnt coat, blackened and charred, flapping in the wind as the demon moved closer with every chasing step.

'Malcolm . . . if you don't go any faster, I'm afraid we're all going to be in trouble,' Hudson pleaded in as gentle a way as possible. 'That bad man is definitely going to catch us.'

The driver looked in his mirror again. 'I'll try, but Mum won't be pleased. Mustn't go faster than thirty on these roads. The Road Patrol Police will come!'

Molly screamed out as Mokee Joe suddenly accelerated. She and Hudson watched helplessly as both back windows smashed and two grasping bony hands poked through and gripped the doorframe.

Without a word, Molly undid her safety belt and jumped over the seat into the back of the van. Striker bounced up and down, barking loudly and snapping in the air at the two clasping hands.

'What's happening?' Malcolm yelled.

'Just keep driving,' Hudson ordered, all sympathy disappearing from his voice. 'Molly, what are you doing?'

Molly didn't answer. She picked up a heavy crowbar placed on the floor of the van, raised it above her shoulder and brought it down across one of the hands gripping the doorframe. The long, bony fingers never moved. She did the same again, but this time struck the other hand. Still no reaction. She screamed as Mokee Joe's hideous scorch-marked face pressed up against one of the broken windows. The eyes, full of evil, stared at the van's occupants. As the eyes finally came to rest on Hudson, the monster's determined expression turned to one of pure hatred.

It was then that Hudson thought about the boxes stacked on the floor. 'Molly – the boxes – take out a couple of jars or bottles or whatever they are and throw them over him.'

As Mokee Joe began tearing at the metal window frames, showers of sparks shooting up from his boots as they trailed on the tarmac, Molly tore frantically at the nearest cardboard box. She snatched up a bottle of yellowish green liquid, unscrewed the top and scattered the contents straight into the face of their enemy. A loud, high-pitched squeal told them that they were gaining the upper hand.

'Yes . . . Moll . . . and again!' Hudson shouted.

Malcolm clung desperately on to the steering wheel and laughed and cried at the same time as Molly picked out another bottle and did the same. The effect was similar, but this time the face and the hand in front of it disappeared. As the van finally reached its top speed of forty-two miles per hour, a loud clang sounded from the rear as Mokee Joe's other hand also disappeared.

Molly shrieked out with glee and Striker barked enthusiastically. 'YYYESSS . . . He's let go!' Hudson watched as she edged up to the broken windows and looked out. 'He's disappeared,' she shouted.

'Has he gone?' Malcolm asked, beads of sweat rolling down his forehead.

'Yes, the bad man's gone,' Hudson sighed with relief. 'But he'll be back, you can be sure of it. Not for you, Malcolm. You're OK. It's me he's after.'

'Can I slow back down to thirty now before the Road Patrol Police come?'

'You can drive at thirty all the way to London if you like,'

Hudson answered, suddenly feeling tired and hungry. He gave a big yawn and looked at Molly. She climbed into the front and sat by his side, yawning back at him.

Malcolm spoke without taking his eyes off the road: 'Have something to eat. Mum will have put you some sandwiches in that bag, and then you can have a sleep. I'll wake you when we get there.'

Hudson thought this was a great idea. He looked into the rucksack and found a plastic container. After he and Molly had eaten a few sandwiches, without daring to ask what was in them, he yawned again and turned to his friend. 'Moll, before I doze off, what was in those bottles you threw over Mokee Joe? Did they contain salt water?'

'I guessed that's what you were thinking,' she answered, reaching over the seat and picking up one of the empty bottles. 'Didn't GA say that Mokee Joe hated the stuff?' Hudson watched as she read the label and then burst into an uncontrollable fit of the giggles.

'What is it, Moll? What does it say?'

'*Jellyfish stings in a suspension of herring urine.* No wonder he let go!'

'Mum will be mad,' Malcolm chipped in as they both laughed together. 'That's her best cure for warts!'

Hudson and Molly laughed even more and Striker wagged his tail and jumped up at them, trying to lick their faces. It was a rare happy moment and they savoured it before they allowed themselves to doze off to sleep.

The van trundled on, finally reaching the motorway, the M20, and headed north towards London.

Malcolm sped up to thirty-five miles per hour and plodded along in the nearside lane feeling disappointed that his back windows had been broken. He worried that the Road Patrol Police might pull him up and ask questions.

Hudson and Molly slept restlessly, their tired bodies trying desperately to regain both physical and mental energy.

Striker lay curled up at Hudson's feet, quietly dozing and throwing in the odd growl here and there. He couldn't understand where or why, but he was the only one who sensed that danger still lurked close to them . . .

6

Road Rage

Hudson had been dozing for some time before the voice of the sea-witch sounded in his head.

'I sense your worry for me, but there is no need. I am quite safe. After delaying the creature for as long as possible I ran and hid in the dunes. He never came after me; he was much too intent on following after you.'

Hudson felt a great wave of relief wash over him knowing that the sea-witch was OK. He concentrated and thought of his reply. 'What about your house? What about your son – so far we've told him nothing?'

'And I thank you for that,' came the response. 'Please don't say anything. He will only worry himself sick. On his return he will help me start again as we have done so many times before. It is not the first time my house has been destroyed. A great storm washed away my first house and took my husband with it. Vandals have since destroyed two more of my houses. So you see, Malcolm and me, we are becoming experts in the art of house rebuilding.'

Hudson sensed the fighting spirit in the sea-witch's words, though he couldn't help feeling sorry for her, as well as for the driver by his side.

The voice continued: 'Remember . . . when you reach London, keep travelling north and west and don't stop until you get back to Danvers Green. You will find some useful items in the bag. I know that you and Molly must be worrying about your parents – they know of your return . . . and are waiting.'

Hudson noticed the hesitation in the sea-witch's voice again.

'And one other thing . . . on your return to Danvers Green you must seek out the Stokeham Professor . . .' But the sea-witch never finished. Her voice faded away as Hudson stirred to full wakefulness.

Molly was still asleep and leaning on his shoulder. Striker snoozed at his feet, but was still making strange noises – a mixture of whining and growling. Malcolm was leaning over the wheel and humming to himself as he concentrated on the road ahead. Hudson noticed that he'd put on a strange sort of baseball cap – it had flaps, which covered his ears.

'Cool cap,' Hudson remarked, but Malcolm didn't reply – he just kept on humming. Hudson raised his voice. 'I LIKE THE CAP.'

Malcolm turned to face him. 'Mum got it me . . . for my

birthday. It's one of the latest SBHs . . . a Sound Byte Hat. I like a bit of music when I'm driving.'

Hudson said nothing. He decided that their driver was definitely 'strange'.

Whilst everything was quiet, Hudson decided to have a look through the rucksack that the sea-witch had given him.

The first thing he found was a large plastic wallet with thirty notes in it. It was obviously money, but the notes looked different – instead of the familiar queen's head, there was a man's head pictured on them and each note had '10E' inside a circle inscribed on both sides. Further into the bag, Hudson found a torch and a pocket watch. He held the watch to his ear – it was ticking. The time on it said 6.15 and Hudson reckoned that was about right – it was already starting to get dark outside. He looked over at the speedometer and saw that the van was only travelling at just under thirty miles per hour – no wonder they'd been on the road such a long time!

Apart from two spare jumpers and a couple of bottles of orange juice, there was nothing much else in the bag. But in the front zip pocket Hudson found a map of London with a diagram of the underground on the back cover. It surprised Hudson that a red circle seemed to label central London as the 'Inner-Zone' and the rest of London as the 'Outer-Zone'. Things were getting stranger by the minute. There was something not quite right.

He thought about the hesitation in the sea-witch's voice and the time back at the old beach hut when she'd avoided eye contact and had seemed guarded. What was she hiding?

Molly yawned and stretched her arms up to the van roof. 'What are you doing?'

'I've been checking out the bag.'

'Hudson, why has this motorway got so many lanes?'

Hudson peered through the windscreen. 'Wow . . . six lanes!' he gasped. 'That's amazing!'

Hudson saw that five of the lanes were full to capacity but the sixth lane, on the very outside, was completely empty. It came as no surprise that *they* were plodding up the inside lane, surrounded by slow-moving lorries and other big vehicles moving along at snail's pace. The outer lanes seemed to contain faster-moving, sleeker cars and some of the makes and designs Hudson failed to recognise.

'Wow! Look at that!' Hudson exclaimed pointing to a long silver streamlined car in the fifth lane. 'It looks like it's just gliding on air.'

Malcolm removed his cap and placed it under the dashboard. 'It's heading for the Inner-Zone – totally electric – don't you know anything?'

Hudson looked at Molly and then they both looked at Malcolm. He looked back at them with an equal amount of puzzlement in his expression.

Before anyone could say anything else, the traffic in the first lane suddenly ground to a halt. Further in front a lorry driver got out, walked around his vehicle and sat on the bonnet.

Malcolm thumped impatiently on the steering wheel. 'Blast! You may as well go back to sleep. That lorry's broken down and we'll probably be stuck here for ages.'

Hudson and Molly stared at each other again in amazement.

'Why doesn't the traffic move over?' Hudson asked.

Malcolm turned and looked at him with a frown. 'You can only go in the lane you're booked in. I'm booked in lane one . . . always 'ave been . . . suppose I always will be!'

'But the lorry's broken down, so surely . . .'

'It's rare that anything breaks down, but when it does, it takes a long time to clear it . . . could be hours.' And saying this, Malcolm took his cap back from under the dashboard, fiddled with something inside it and placed it back on his head. He started humming to himself again.

Molly reached back and adjusted her ponytail. 'Hudson . . . what's going on?'

Hudson didn't reply. He stared forward, deep in thought. She grabbed hold of Hudson's sleeve and tugged at the blue material. 'I mean these school uniforms are definitely a bit weird and since when have motorways looked like this.'

Before Hudson could reply, a strange scraping noise sounded from the underside of the van and Striker got to his feet and growled.

'What's that?' Molly asked with a worried look on her face. 'Don't tell me *we're* breaking down now?'

Hudson's heart began to beat faster. He sensed all was not well – especially with the way that Striker was behaving. His head began to ache – a sure warning that his enemy might be around. He looked back out of the broken rear window. The traffic stretched back in their lane in an endless queue. Meanwhile, the traffic in the other lanes glided on past. It was all so frustrating. But at least there was no sign of Mokee Joe.

While the wait went on, Hudson told Molly about the message he'd received from the sea-witch and how she'd said their parents were waiting for them. He also told Molly about the contents of the bag – about the strange money and the other things.

'Well at least it sounds as if things are OK in Danvers Green,' Molly said, feeling slightly reassured. 'But I still think we should find a phone and contact our parents as soon as we get to London – just to check that they're OK. Right now – I know it sounds silly – but I'd like to ask Malcolm what date it is.'

Hudson watched as she prodded an elbow into Malcolm's side so that he took off his cap again. 'Sorry to interrupt your music, but what date is it?'

He gave her a strange look. 'Don't you know – it's Wednesday!'

'Yes . . . but what year?' Molly asked impatiently.

She and Hudson watched his face contort into a look of bewilderment. He scratched his chin, stretched out his left hand and started counting on his fingers. He scratched his chin again and then smiled triumphantly. 'Two thousand and . . .'

Somewhere above the roof of the van a deafening whirring sound drowned out his reply. As Hudson and Molly leaned forward and strained to see up into the sky, a huge helicopter appeared in front of them. It was a striking yellow colour with the letters MBU painted in black along both sides.

'Hooray! Shouldn't be too long,' Malcolm exclaimed loudly.

The two friends watched in amazement as the helicopter hovered above the broken-down lorry and a moment later five thick cables dropped down to the road. Four of the cables had some sort of hooks on the end. The fifth cable had a man clinging to the end dressed in a uniform the same colour as the helicopter. He also had the letters MBU written on his back.

'What does MBU stand for?' Hudson asked.

'Motorway Breakdown Unit,' Malcolm answered in a tone that suggested Hudson really should have known.

The man in the uniform attached four of the cables to the four corners of the lorry and signalled the driver to get back in the cab. After grabbing hold of the fifth cable and being winched back up to the helicopter, Hudson and Molly watched in disbelief as the lorry was suddenly hoisted up and swung away. The helicopter and its broken-down cargo disappeared rapidly into the distance and as it did so, the traffic in the nearside lane started to move again. The scraping noise under the van stopped and everyone settled down for the final stage of the journey.

* * *

The M20 narrowed into the A20, the A20 continued into the A2 and finally, as they entered Borough High Street, Malcolm announced that they were almost there.

Hudson looked at the pocket watch. It was dark now and he struggled to see it – just after 7.45 pm. He put it into the trouser pocket of his 'school uniform' and decided he was glad he didn't have to drive for a living. The journey had seemed to take an eternity. He would be more than pleased to get out of the van and into the fresh air. Though looking at the heaving traffic and the fumes, he wondered just how fresh the air would be.

'Just up here . . .' Malcolm announced, '. . . there's a tube station on the left, up by these traffic lights. If the lights are on stop there should be time for you to hop out. I'm going further on into the zone-barrier underground car park. It's just a short taxi ride from there.'

'Won't the hospital delivery place be closed?' Molly asked, gazing out of the window into the busy street. The streams of car headlights and bright street lamps were dazzling.

'No . . . Derek lives in a flat on the premises. We'll be going out for a drink later. But you two must be careful . . . Mum wouldn't like it . . . me leaving you in the dark . . . some funny people around!'

Hudson and Molly looked at each other. Neither could disagree with that!

Hudson saw the sign for the tube station and grabbed his bag. Molly slipped off her seatbelt. Striker looked up at Hudson and whined. And then he panted hard, as if trying to tell him something.

'What's wrong, boy?'

The lights were on green so Malcolm couldn't stop. 'Don't worry, just the other side of the lights I can swing into Angel Court. I'll drop you there and you can walk back.'

As the van rattled its way through the busy junction, Hudson stared at the impressive church in the middle of the road. Everything seemed infinitely bigger and busier than Danvers Green.

By some miracle, Malcolm managed to swing the old van across the road into a narrow alleyway. He stopped, facing some black wrought iron railings with an open gate leading into a yard.

'OK, I'll just pull through the gate and turn round in that

courtyard, and then you can be on your way. Just head back down to the tube station. It's a bit grotty in there – still in the Outer-Zone, but one stop down the line you can change at the Elephant and Castle and head into the Inner-Zone – and then Mum said something about Paddington.'

Hudson had already got his route worked out. 'OK, thanks,' he said, grabbing the straps of the rucksack again.

They waited for the van to move forward through the gate, but though the engine revved up, nothing happened. 'Something's wrong,' Malcolm groaned. He pressed on the accelerator again. Still the van didn't move. Striker began to bark loudly.

'Something's definitely wrong,' Hudson shouted, putting a hand to the side of his head. 'I don't know how, but Mokee Joe's responsible. I can feel his presence, and so can Striker.'

'But we left him miles back,' Molly replied, instinctively looking over her shoulder. And then she screamed, 'HUDSON – HE'S BEHIND US!'

They all swung round and watched in horror as Mokee Joe lifted the back of the van and raised it high off the floor. Hudson almost slipped off his seat. 'That's why the van won't move. He's lifting the back wheels off the ground.'

Malcolm still couldn't understand what was happening and pressed even harder on the accelerator. At the same time, Mokee Joe dropped the van and as the wheels hit the floor it shot forward out of control and smashed into the iron railings by the side of the gate.

Hudson thrust the passenger door open and tumbled out. Molly and Striker followed and they all landed in a heap on the tarmac. Mokee Joe stood about five metres back with his fists raised and a look of triumph on his evil face.

A voice screamed from inside the cab. 'BAD MAN BACK! HE BROKE MY WINDOWS AND TWO OF MUM'S POTIONS. IT'S PAY-BACK TIME!'

Without another word, Malcolm revved up the engine so hard that it sounded as if it was going to explode. He crashed the gears into reverse and set off backwards, steam still hissing from the damaged radiator.

Hudson and Molly looked back and saw Mokee Joe moving slowly towards them, glowing electric blue in the gloom of the narrow alleyway. They watched in horror as he raised his bony fingers ready to unleash a charge of electricity. *He was so intent on his target that he never saw the back of the old van until it was too late.*

It slammed into his charred raincoat so that he finished up firmly back where Hudson worked out he had just come from – underneath the floor of the vehicle!

'GO! GET OUT OF HERE! YOU NEED TO GET AWAY! MUM SAID!'

With Malcolm's voice ringing in their ears, and the sight of Mokee Joe's seven-foot frame wrestling to get out from under the wrecked van, Hudson, Molly and Striker tore off down the High Street, back towards Borough Underground Station.

But as Hudson took a last look, just to check that Malcolm had got away and was in no danger, his heart skipped a beat.

Mokee Joe was already on his feet and hurtling after them.

7

'Moll, I've never been near an underground station before. How about you?' Hudson yelled as they approached the tube station.

'Yes – two years ago – for my tenth birthday – Mum and Dad brought me to London for the day. We'll need to get through the ticket barrier.'

The sound of screeching brakes, screaming and yelling from behind and car horns sounding everywhere told them that Mokee Joe was hot on their heels.

Hudson's leg was completely cured and he was the first to turn into the station and see the metal barriers. 'JUST GET OVER . . . THERE'S NO TIME TO PAY!' he screamed over his shoulder.

Hudson leapt over the barrier easily, but as he turned he saw that Molly was out of breath and struggling. He reached back, grabbed her hand and lifted her over the metal bars. Striker simply shot underneath.

'Hey, man, what's your game?' an attendant shouted from over by the pay kiosk.

'Sorry!' Hudson yelled back as the three of them disappeared around the corner.

Next, they came face to face with a lift – fortunately, the shiny metal doors were open and they leapt inside.

But the doors were slow to close.

Frightened screams from around the corner told them that Mokee Joe was almost upon them. The doors still didn't close.

'Oh my God, Hudson. He'll be here any second.'

Just as the horrible spectre of their enemy came into view the doors finally started to close, but only slowly. Striker growled and jumped through the gap, ready to fight, but Hudson quickly grabbed his collar and yanked him back. At the same time, Mokee Joe leapt forward and thrust his hand in between the doors – just as they finally hissed shut. His great pincer-like hand was trapped, the doors jammed and the lift refused to move.

'Hudson, he's going to get in!' Molly yelled. She clenched her fist and struck a blow at the clawing fingers. But it was she who winced, 'OUCH!' The hand never moved.

'OK, let's see what I can do!' Hudson yelled. Repeating Molly's action he brought his arm back and struck a mighty blow at Mokee Joe's wriggling hand.

The steel doors shook under the force and this time there

was a reaction. The hand shot back and disappeared. The gap closed and the lift finally began its descent.

'That was a close one,' Hudson sighed. 'We're going to have to move more quickly.'

'I can't go much faster,' Molly panted, picking up Striker. The little dog was also panting. He let out a little whine and licked her face.

A moment later, the lift doors opened and they stepped out into a gloomy passage. It was almost circular, covered in original Victorian black and white tiles, most of them cracked. The walls curved away from them and Hudson ran on, shouting at Molly to follow. The passage had an air of decay, dusty wires and cables straggling overhead. Hudson kept looking back, dreading the prospect of seeing Mokee Joe close on their heels, but the curved walls made it impossible to see if anything was following.

A flight of steps appeared. They leapt down them and found themselves standing on the platform by the side of the rails. Hudson looked around in awe.

To his left, a few people stood waiting, one or two of them wearing executive-looking suits and carrying briefcases. To his right, his eyes followed the rail tracks into the blackness of the circular tunnel, a single small green light showing from deep within. A strange current of air came out of the passage and brushed by his head making a ghostly moaning sound.

'Moll, this place is so weird.'

Molly cradled Striker in her arms and shivered. 'I know. Places like this give me the creeps. Do you think Mokee Joe has found the emergency stairs yet?'

Before Hudson could reply, a rumbling, roaring sound

filled his ears and everything seemed to rattle and shake as a train shot out from the blackness and slowed to a halt. The carriages were all daubed with graffiti. Only the streamlined driver's carriage at the front suggested any hint of modern technology.

A handful of people got off and a moment later, as the three fugitives dashed on board, loud screams sounded from close by.

'WATCH OUT – HE'S HERE!' Molly shrieked, pointing up the platform. Thankfully, the doors were already closing and the train pulling away . . . straight towards the demonic figure.

A few seconds later, Hudson shielded his face as Mokee Joe swung an angry fist at the window of their passing carriage. The glass cracked from top to bottom, but it didn't smash. Passengers still on the platform fled screaming in every direction. A woman by Hudson's side fainted as the other passengers inside looked on in awe.

'We've made it, Hudson. At least for the time being. We're away again,' Molly sighed. She put Striker down on the floor.

Hudson didn't reply at first. He stared forward, deep in concentration. It was a good few seconds before he answered. 'Sorry, Moll. I wish you were right, but we're not rid of Mokee Joe yet. I'll hold Striker this time. As soon as the train stops I want you to follow me – we'll need to run for our lives.'

Molly went a funny sort of pale colour. 'Why, Hudson? Where is he?'

As the train bumped and jolted and slowed towards the next station, Hudson answered in as calm a voice as he could manage: '*He's clinging to the back of the train.*'

* * *

An automated voice sounded in the compartment: '*The next station will be the Elephant and Castle.*'

Hudson turned to Molly. 'We're going to get off. Are you ready?'

'As ready as I'll ever be,' Molly answered, biting her bottom lip.

Just before the doors had fully opened they took a deep breath and a second later they were out. Hudson looked quickly up the platform and saw the 'Way Out' sign. Molly was already running towards it.

'NO . . . STOP!' Hudson yelled.

He turned and looked in the other direction, down the platform, towards the back of the train, and saw the sign he was looking for – another 'Way Out' sign, but underneath it an arrow pointing towards the Bakerloo Line. 'We need to go that way.'

'But we can't,' Molly shrieked. 'You said he's on the back of the train.'

As if to confirm Molly's statement, they watched in horror as their demon pursuer jumped out from the rear of the carriage and stood in defiance on the platform. A man wearing a pinstriped suit, who happened to be passing, dropped his briefcase and bolted towards the exit. But Mokee Joe didn't give him a second look.

The doors of the train started to close as it prepared to pull away.

Hudson, still carrying Striker under one arm, grabbed Molly with the other. 'QUICK! GET BACK ON!'

As they leapt back through the doors, Mokee Joe reacted

by jumping back on to the rear of the train – just as Hudson predicted.

Before Molly had chance to ask Hudson what he was up to, he handed her the dog and as the train pulled away he used his strength to force the doors apart. 'TRUST ME, MOLLY – JUMP THROUGH THE GAP!' In disbelief she did as she was told and as Hudson followed they all finished up in a heap back on the platform.

'Hudson . . . what . . .'

But before she could finish her question, the back of the train sped past – and Molly gasped as she saw their enemy still clinging to the back of the rear carriage glowering with rage . . .

Now they were free to run towards the exit that linked up with the Bakerloo Line.

As Mokee Joe realised he'd been tricked, he screamed a high-pitched electronic scream and threw himself off the accelerating train. He landed at the opposite end of the platform in a crumpled heap.

Hudson took a last look over his shoulder and watched as a stunned station official moved in a challenging way towards the prostrate body. But as Mokee Joe regained his stance, the man thought better of it and fled out of the far exit.

'OK! LET'S GO . . . WE DON'T HAVE A SECOND TO LOSE. HE'S STILL ON OUR TAIL!'

If the last tube station was old and spooky, the Elephant and Castle was worse.

The passage leading to the Bakerloo Line curved away again, this time adorned in cracked, yellowed tiles, edged in deep red – almost the colour of blood, Hudson thought to himself. Somewhere ahead, a saxophone played a mournful tune. Close behind, the frightening ring of heavy chasing footsteps echoed around the passage.

They ran on, terrified of taking a wrong turning.

More than once, Hudson thought he could hear the sound of electricity crackling through the air behind them, but he never looked back – every second was precious.

They reached a shabbily dressed, middle-aged man sitting on the floor half way down one of the passages . . . the saxophone player. Hudson screamed at him to get up and run.

The musician stopped playing for a second, but only so he could mutter curses at them. And then he carried on his mournful tune.

They ran on, and just as they emerged out of the passage on to the Bakerloo Line, the sound of the saxophone stopped abruptly. A shrill scream followed and as it echoed up the passage they knew that Mokee Joe was almost upon them.

As luck would have it, a train had just pulled in. They leapt on board and prayed the doors would close quickly. They did. But as the train pulled away, the menacing, angry figure of Mokee Joe appeared once more. More screams and yells rang out as people fled in all directions.

Hudson watched his enemy run towards the rear.

'He's getting on the back again, isn't he?' Molly asked with frightened eyes. 'We can't seem to shake him off.'

'I know,' was all Hudson said.

'This is even worse than before. He just seems to keep on coming. I'm frightened, Hudson.'

Hudson looked at Molly's worried expression. Striker jumped down, gazed up at her and wagged his tail. Even he could sense she was upset.

Molly rarely admitted she was scared of anything and it upset Hudson to hear her say it. But truthfully, he was just as scared as she was.

The train sped on towards Paddington with Mokee Joe presumably still clinging to the back and Hudson racking his brain trying to think what to do next.

As the underground train moved on, passing through Waterloo and Embankment, Hudson kept his mind clear of thoughts. He had a definite ache in his head and he guessed that Mokee Joe was trying to read his mind. At Charing Cross a number of policemen appeared on the platform. They seemed agitated. They moved towards the back of the train as it ground to a halt.

'Hudson, look! They must have found out about him riding on the back of the train.'

As Molly spoke, Striker, who was sitting at her feet, suddenly tilted his head and started barking up at the roof of the carriage.

'Striker knows what's going off,' Hudson whispered in her ear. 'Mokee Joe's right above us. He's been working himself along the top of the train ever since we changed back at the Elephant and Castle. The police will never spot him. When we try to get off, he'll jump down and strike.'

'So what'll we do?'

'Trust me. I'll think of something.'

The train pulled away again, the police looking puzzled

and no doubt thinking they'd been the victims of a hoax. *After all*, Hudson thought to himself, *it's not every day that a seven-foot monster is reported hitching a ride on the back of a tube train!*

'So we'll risk it. We'll get off at Paddington and then from there we'll catch a proper train,' Hudson said for the tenth time as they pulled into Piccadilly Circus.

'Hudson, why do you keep on repeating yourself? Are you OK?'

'Sorry, Moll,' Hudson apologised with a strained look on his face.

The train doors slid open. 'And I'm sorry about this as well . . .' He picked up Striker and started counting to himself. 'One, two, three, four, five, six . . .' and as the doors started to close he pushed Molly out on to the Piccadilly platform and jumped off after her. Hudson had timed his move with absolute precision, but from Molly's point of view it was totally unexpected and she landed in a heap on the cold concrete.

As the train pulled away, Hudson and Molly looked up above the doors and saw the elongated body of their enemy stretched out on the roof . . . demonic eyes staring out of the darkness . . . an expression of pure frustration. They just managed to hear the high-pitched scream of anger above the roar of the train as it disappeared into the blackness of the tunnel.

Molly stood up, dusted herself down and rubbed the top of her left leg where she'd landed heavily. 'Hudson, that really hurt! What were you up to?'

'He was reading my mind, Moll. I had to convince him we were going on to Paddington – that's why I kept telling you – to keep the real plan out of my mind. And it worked. We're here and he's gone. And this time he can't get off, at least not until the next station.'

Striker barked up at Hudson, as if in admiration. Molly reached down and patted the dog's head affectionately.

'Brilliant, Hudson. I should never have doubted you. Really brilliant!'

A tremendous wave of relief washed over the two friends as they made their way out from the underground. They travelled up two steep escalators, and on towards the exit. At the surface barriers, Hudson approached the attendant and told them he'd lost their tickets. The man frowned, winked at him and let them through. 'You're not the first kids to try that one,' the man laughed. 'Don't try it again . . . at least not with me, anyway!'

Hudson looked at Molly and they both managed to force a smile.

Once through the barriers, there were lots of different stairways rising up to Piccadilly Circus. Hudson chose one with a sign that said 'Lower Regent Street' and 'Eros' beneath it. 'What does "Eros" mean, Moll?' Hudson asked as they made their way up into the cool night air.

'It's that statue, the one with the bow . . . there!' She pointed to a circle of steps capped with the impressive figure of an archer. As they walked over and sat on the steps, Hudson gazed round with his mouth wide open.

Bright lights shone out from everywhere. There were even some strange lights moving in the night sky overhead. They glided and hovered like giant moths and Hudson couldn't work out what they were.

All around, tall impressive buildings closed in on everything, their facades covered with dazzling illuminated advertisements. Over to his left, on top of one of the highest buildings, a huge electronic screen displayed a blaze of animated colour.

Even at this late hour the traffic was heavy, though surprisingly quiet. And then Hudson noticed that all the cars were long and streamlined, like the ones he'd seen travelling in the outer lanes of the motorway. Hadn't Malcolm said something about them being 'Inner-Zone' cars and all electric?

'Wow, Moll – this is so amazing. I can't believe it . . . it . . . it's like another planet!'

'Well you should know,' Molly giggled. 'Hudson, pass me some money. It's time we ate. I'll get something for us from that kiosk over there and I'll just pay a visit to the loo at the same time.'

Hudson unzipped a pocket in the rucksack and rooted around.

Ten minutes later both he and Molly had been to the loo and were tucking into chicken salad sandwiches. Striker joined in the feast. He was just as ravenous as they were.

A party of Chinese students arrived and sat by them, drinking bottles of Coke and chatting enthusiastically. They looked up at the moving display boards and seemed just as fascinated by them as Hudson.

Hudson began to relax. He finished his sandwich and

gazed up at the huge advertising hoarding on top of the building again. Ever since they'd first sat down, a cartoon boy on some sort of jet-propelled skateboard had been speeding from left to right advertising 'Rocky Rocketboards'. But now, for the first time, Hudson saw something else. As the electronic writing moved across the screen from left to right, Hudson went numb with shock and began to choke on his sandwich.

'Hudson! What's wrong?' Molly asked, slapping him on the back.

'Nothing . . . just a bit of bread going down the wrong way.'

Molly mustn't see it . . . not yet, Hudson thought to himself.

He looked up again, allowed his eyes to roll backwards and concentrated all his mental energy on to the screen.

Molly stared at him – it wasn't the first time she'd seen Hudson like this. And then she followed his gaze and saw that the screen had stopped working . . . as if the power had gone off.

'Hudson . . . what are you doing?' she whispered.

The Chinese students muttered in disappointment. Molly glanced around at them and then several of them pointed up and laughed out excitedly. Molly looked back to the screen and almost fainted.

A new cartoon had appeared.

Three animated figures – a boy with a familiar hairstyle, a girl with a ponytail and a small dog – ran across the screen being chased by a tall, familiar monster.

Molly shrieked out in surprise as the students laughed out loud. Even Striker seemed to recognise himself. He looked up and barked towards the screen, wagging his tail.

'Hudson, you're amazing,' Molly said, pulling on his arm. 'How do you do that?'

Hudson concentrated a while longer and then snapped himself out of his trance. The screen went blank again. A few seconds later, much to everyone's disappointment, 'Rocky Rocketboards' made a reappearance.

Hudson changed the subject away from the screen. 'I'll just have a study of the map, Moll, and then we ought to be on our way.'

He rooted around in the bag, desperate to keep Molly's attention. He took out the torch and the London map, studied the map for a few minutes and then made ready to go.

'Not back on the tube again?' Molly sighed.

Hudson scratched his chin.

On his left he noticed a theatre with an ominous crest above its entrance – a spooky head, some sort of devil, leering down at him. Suddenly, like Molly, he didn't really feel like going back down into the underground.

'No, not for the time being. We'll stay above ground. By my reckoning we need to head off across the road, up Regent Street and on towards Portland Place and Regent's Park. If we feel up to it, we can go back on the underground there and take the tube into Paddington.'

Molly jumped up. 'I'm going to find a phone first and ring Mum.'

One of the students, sitting by Molly's side, overheard and smiled at her. 'I haven't heard anyone use words like "ring" or "phone" for a long time. Where are you from?'

'Danvers Green,' Molly replied sheepishly.

'Well, if you give me your mother's zone code and number I'll zap her for you now if you like.' The student looked down at a metal band on his wrist and started fiddling with it.

Molly was lost for words. She looked at Hudson. But he only sat there with his mouth open. 'Er . . . it's OK. I'll try her later,' was all she could think to say.

The student got up to leave. 'Fine . . . good luck.'

Hudson stood up – he really needed to get Molly away – he needed time to think. 'Come on, Moll. Let's move on.' He pointed across the road towards a sign that read 'Regent Street' and they set off towards it.

Just before crossing the road, Hudson took a final sneaky look up at the big electronic screen. He'd certainly impressed Molly with his 'thought projection' trick – though it had taken an enormous amount of energy.

Just before his eyes left the screen, the Rocky Rocketboards boy disappeared and it went blank again. But this time, Hudson knew he wasn't responsible.

To Hudson's horror, Molly turned and stared upwards as a new message glided across from left to right:

Nowhere is safe . . .
MJ

'It couldn't be from him, could it?' Molly asked, sensing Hudson's train of thought.

'I think it could . . .' Hudson replied quickly. 'Come on, let's go.'

As they walked off, the screen filled up with new information – the same devastating information that Hudson had seen earlier . . . he glanced over his shoulder and led Molly away before she had chance to see it:

21:05

5 degrees Celsius

Thursday 24th March **2025**

8

Alternative Transport

Two lonely figures and a small dog made their way up Regent Street.

The electronic message in Piccadilly Circus had been like a double-edged blade. Hudson was trying to get his head around the fact that they had somehow found themselves twenty years in the future. And if Mokee Joe's warning that 'Nowhere is safe!' had been designed to put his and Molly's nerves on edge and sink their spirits, then it had most definitely succeeded.

Hudson looked around in awe at the vast scale of his surroundings and wondered how many hiding places were available for his enemy to lie in ambush. Molly looked tired and dragged behind him, all the time looking nervously in one direction and then the other. Even Striker seemed to have his senses on full alert. He raced ahead, constantly sniffing the pavement and investigating every turning and alleyway.

The 'silent' traffic began to thin a little and there were not so many people about. It was getting late and Hudson started thinking about last trains from Paddington.

They put a spurt on, moving on beyond another huge church in the middle of the road, continuing along Portland Place past some very impressive hotels, and then on towards Regent's Park.

As they crossed over on to Marylebone Road Hudson glanced at the pocket watch whilst Molly sat down on the edge of the kerb.

'How much further, Hudson? I'm exhausted.'

He looked down at her tired expression. How was he going to tell her about the date? He knew she'd be devastated. But she had to know . . . perhaps when they got to the station and were sitting comfortably on the train . . . 'If we go back underground and take the tube it'll be minutes, but it's still a good way if we walk.'

'I really don't like the idea of going back down there,' Molly said nervously. Striker jumped up at her and gave a little whimper. 'See . . . even he agrees.'

Hudson looked thoughtful. He took his rucksack off his back and passed it to Molly.

'OK. Put Striker in this. Zip it up so his head's sticking out and then put it on. You two are going for a ride.'

Molly and Striker were so tired that neither objected. The little Jack Russell allowed Molly to place him in the canvas bag and then she slipped the straps over her shoulders as Hudson had instructed.

'But where's the transport?' she asked. 'Are we going to flag a taxi?'

'No time . . .' Hudson replied mysteriously. 'Now get on!'

He turned his back to her, bent his legs, lowered his hands by his side and made ready to give her a piggyback.

'You're joking!' Molly gasped in disbelief. She took a last look at Striker to make sure he was comfortable, jumped on Hudson's back and prepared for anything.

Within seconds, Striker was barking excitedly and Molly was shrieking with glee as Hudson ran off up the road accelerating rapidly.

A late night cyclist, out taking advantage of London's quieter night-time roads, appeared ahead of them. His helmet, clothes and cycle were the ultimate in streamlined design and he pedalled on with head down at an impressive speed. As Hudson and his two passengers approached Baker Street they sprinted past him. Molly looked back and laughed out loud as the cyclist wobbled to a halt in a complete state of shock.

Within five minutes, Hudson arrived at Paddington Station. Molly and Striker had had the ride of their lives.

'Hudson – you never fail to amaze me!' Molly said, taking the bag off her shoulders and lifting Striker down on to the floor. 'What else can you do?'

'That's just it, Moll. I don't know,' Hudson answered modestly. This was the second time he'd impressed Molly that evening and it cheered him up a little. 'GA said my powers are just about fully developed, but I'm learning all the time.'

'Well, I'm staggered – it's unreal. You'll be able to fly next.'

Hudson thought back to the time he'd left his body and flown across Danvers Green to visit GA. It was the most exciting thing that had ever happened to him. 'Maybe . . . who knows?' he said modestly.

As they made their way into the biggest station he or Molly had ever seen, Hudson scanned around cautiously.

A few passengers scurried back and forth and a number of station staff were evident, some guiding electrically operated trolleys loaded up with luggage and various other items. A few cleaning staff were also around and two black ladies wearing white overalls and face masks were each carrying a mop and bucket towards the toilet area. Two trains were waiting at adjacent platforms. The trains were silver and streamlined and, like the underground carriages, covered in graffiti. They were like nothing Hudson had ever seen before.

But at least, despite these observations, nothing seemed untoward or threatening.

Molly had also been scanning around. 'No sign of you-know-who?' she whispered.

'No.'

A man in some sort of station porter's uniform ambled towards them.

'A bit late for young kids to be out on their own?' the man said gruffly. 'Where are your parents? I hope you two haven't run away from home?'

'No, nothing like that,' Hudson replied, his brain thinking quickly, 'but we should have been home hours ago. That's why we're in a hurry. Mum will probably have the police out by now.'

As Hudson spoke, he observed one of the electric trolleys piled high with suitcases coming up behind the man.

'Well, all the same, I don't like to see young kids out on their own at this time of night. You never know who's around . . .'

Hudson stared over the man's shoulder as the tower of suitcases loomed up behind him. The cases were stacked much too high and looked precarious. The station official was completely oblivious. He raised his arm and adjusted a metal band on his wrist. He was about to speak into it when the inevitable happened. The trolley pulled up behind him and the huge pile of suitcases collapsed almost giving him a heart attack. But when he and Hudson and Molly saw who was pushing the trolley, they all yelled out in terror.

In the middle of the pool of scattered suitcases, Mokee Joe stood in all his nightmarish glory!

The station official stood rooted to the spot and offered no resistance as the seven-foot monster brushed him callously to one side.

Striker growled and went straight for the demon's ankles, but Mokee Joe ignored the animal and made a grab for Hudson.

The 'piggyback journey' had left Hudson weak and before he had time to react, Mokee Joe picked him up and threw him with great force five metres into a metal upright. Hudson braced himself as his body struck the pole with a great CLANG and then he sank into a limp sitting position on the floor, stars magically appearing before his eyes. To make matters worse, his enemy then raised a bony hand and unleashed an electric charge – it struck the metal pole and conducted down into Hudson's body. The pain was searing and unbearable – he thought he was about to die.

Molly, meanwhile, had already dashed off to the left and snatched up one of the cleaning lady's buckets.

As Mokee Joe glowered triumphantly in Hudson's direction, Molly unleashed a mixture of disinfectant and dirty water over the back of his unsuspecting head. A blinding blue flash ensued and the monster reeled to face his new attacker. He screamed a chilling high-pitched scream and danced with rage as his black felt hat hissed and smoked.

But Molly was having none of it!

She jabbed the monster full in the face with the heavy mop and a further discharge of dirty liquid washed over Mokee Joe's grotesque head. All the time Striker was clinging to his trouser bottoms and desperately trying to sink his fangs into the steel-like ankles.

Mokee Joe screamed again and staggered backwards, but he was still far from overpowered. He kicked his leg out so hard that Striker was flung across the ground. At the same time he snatched the mop from Molly's grasp and snapped the handle into two halves as if it was matchwood. One of the halves had a lethal-looking point and the monster pulled his arm back and prepared to use it like a spear.

But Molly's distraction had given Hudson time to recover. His body had quickly regained its strength. He jumped to his feet and snatched a nearby trolley, deserted moments earlier by one of the terrified staff. As he took hold of the handle it automatically clicked into gear and edged forward. Hudson felt his muscles surge as he pushed and accelerated the trolley towards the back of Mokee Joe's legs.

Just as the creature's arm prepared to unleash its deadly javelin, the trolley arrived at tremendous speed and took his legs from under him. Molly dived out of the way as the trolley and its grotesque cargo hurtled past.

Screaming passengers, shocked station staff and terrified cleaning ladies watched in disbelief as the trolley crashed with tremendous force into the wall at the top of a steep flight of steps leading down into the gents' loo. But if the trolley was too wide to fit through the open doorway, much to Hudson and Molly's delight, Mokee Joe's gangly frame was not.

The two friends watched in fascination as their enemy disappeared with a tremendous crash down the steep steps. But Hudson knew there was no time to gloat.

Striker, though shaken, was already back by their feet. Molly snatched him up as Hudson screamed at her, 'QUICK . . . FOLLOW ME.'

With everyone's attention on the toilet area, hardly anyone took any notice of the boy and a girl carrying a dog and running towards the two waiting trains.

Hudson looked up at an electronic screen at the entrance to the first platform. It was headed with 'Great Western Link'. He ran on towards the next train and this time the screen was headed 'North Western Link'. That sounded good. The train began to hiss louder in a way that suggested it was about to leave. The three fugitives ran alongside, jumped on board and found themselves in an empty carriage. Hudson slumped on to one seat and Molly sprawled across a seat on the opposite side of the aisle. The train doors hissed shut and the train glided silently away.

Hudson had never felt such relief. For the time being they were safe again and hopefully travelling in the right direction.

'Wow . . . that was a close one. We could have been killed back there,' Hudson said, running his hand through his hair.

Striker curled up on the floor at Molly's feet. 'You're right,' she said, 'we could have been killed. But then anything could have happened . . . I don't know what's real any more and what isn't. I mean . . . have you ever seen trains like these before and what about all the other goings-on? That motorway, for example . . . and did you know that back in Piccadilly, when I bought those sandwiches, I didn't even understand the money? The woman had to take it from me and count it – like I was some sort of moron. And when I asked her what date it was she said it's the twenty-fourth of March. Then when I asked her what year it was she just laughed and decided I really was a moron. For heaven's sake, Hudson . . . what's happening to us?'

Hudson took a deep breath. He didn't like keeping secrets from his best friend. It was time to tell her the awful truth.

Molly saw the strained look on his face. 'For God's sake, Hudson . . . what's up?' she stammered.

But before Hudson could find the words to reply, a screen directly above the door of their compartment burst into life. They both looked up, as the holographic image of an attractive woman's face projected itself out of the screen and began to speak.

'*Welcome to the North Western Link.*

This train is destined for the following municipalities: Uxbridge, Beaconsfield, High Wycombe, Stokenchurch, Wheatley and Oxford Central.

We hope you will have a pleasant journey. Please have your zone passes ready.

The current time is twenty-two thirty hours on the twenty-fourth of March, **two thousand and twenty-five** *.'*

Hudson watched helplessly as Molly's mouth fell open. He put his fingers to his ears as the scream came out from her throat and echoed around the compartment. Finally, he went over and put his arm around her as she began to shake like a leaf and sob in a way he would never have believed possible.

But at least now Molly knew the truth.

And Hudson needed her support just as much as she needed his in facing up to the mind-blowing fact that they had somehow found themselves projected over twenty years into the future!

9

ALL HALLOWS COLLEGE

Place of Learning

The train sped on in a north-westerly direction towards Oxford.

Molly had cried quietly and drifted off to sleep. Striker remained curled up at her feet making a strange sort of doggy snoring noise. Hudson sat quietly by her side, going over and over the shocking implications that the recent news had presented to them.

If the year was 2025 then Mr and Mrs Brown, Hudson's adoptive parents, must be well into their seventies. They may not even be alive. No wonder the sea-witch had sounded anxious on the subject of contacting parents – she had doubtless been aware of their awful situation. Molly had worked out that both her parents would be in their late fifties and this had greatly upset her . . . so many years of their lives lost to her for ever . . . and her Labrador, Sampson, would have died years ago. So would Pugwash, Hudson's cat . . . it didn't bear thinking about. And what about Ash and all their friends from school? They would be adults – grown up and probably married . . .

Molly was now more desperate than ever to contact home. Before she'd fallen asleep she'd insisted that as soon as they got off the train she was going to find out how to get in touch with her parents. But Hudson had managed to calm her down and persuade her to trust in his judgement. If he and Molly had been missing for twenty years, what difference would a couple more days make? And what about the shock to their parents? It was important to try to see things from their point of view . . . perhaps this was why the sea-witch had been so hesitant.

Molly had solemnly nodded her head as Hudson had summarised their situation.

Their mission was to lead Mokee Joe back to Danvers Green. This was their destiny. GA had made that clear and Hudson trusted in his late uncle's judgement one hundred per cent. The sea-witch had told Hudson to get in touch with the Stokeham Professor. Who *he* was he didn't have a clue, but in some way Hudson sensed that this meeting might lead to a possible solution in dealing with a seemingly impossible situation – to rid himself of his enemy once and for all.

And where was Mokee Joe now?

As Molly dozed on and the train passed through several stations and on into the night, a dull throb around Hudson's temples told him that his enemy was very much alive and still trying to tune in to his whereabouts. And the more he tried to keep the word 'Oxford' out of his thoughts, the more it seemed to come up in his mind.

He remembered GA's dying words; that he was now almost fully developed and strong in body and mind, but Hudson knew only too well that he was still young and inexperienced – nowhere near as mentally strong as his uncle. He still wasn't able to fully block out his thoughts and stop Mokee Joe from getting into his head.

No – one thing was for certain – Mokee Joe would soon be back on their trail!

With all these thoughts racing around in his brain, Hudson moved back to the seat across the aisle and leaned his head up against the cool glass of the window. He strained to see outside, but it was too dark, he couldn't see anything – no lights, no moon and no stars – just his own faint reflection staring back from within the darkened glass.

The high-tech train sped smoothly over the rails and there was little vibration, but as Hudson focused on his image and he began to see his features more clearly, the sight of his head continuously nodding back and forth had a strangely hypnotic effect.

Suddenly, without any warning, the calming image changed and Hudson found himself staring straight into the eyes of Mokee Joe!

He recoiled in horror as the demon face glowered back at him.

And then Hudson read the expression on the grotesque features and understood what the projected image of his enemy was saying . . . that he could see Hudson . . . that he knew where he was and where he was going . . . that it was only a matter of time before he caught up with him . . . *and then . . .!*

Hudson decided to retaliate. He took a deep breath, sat up straight and stared back in defiance. He concentrated all his mental energy towards the glass, emptied his mind of all fearful thoughts and replaced them with the words: *I will not rest until you are destroyed!*

The dreadful image sneered back at him and then slowly faded away – but only to be replaced with a different reflection!

Hudson watched in disbelief as a second face materialised in the dark glass. As it became clearer, he saw that it had sharp cheekbones, a broad toothy grin and a turban on its head.

And this image projected a friendly feel so that Hudson relaxed a little.

The face continued to smile and Hudson sensed it wanted to communicate. Confident that his enemy had gone, he opened his mind and allowed the new thought waves to flow in.

Hi . . . it's very nice to meet you. I hope that your senses are telling you that you can trust me . . . I am firmly on your side and here to help you. I'll be waiting for you at Oxford and we can take it from there.

The sparkling eyes oozed intelligence and the sense of caring coming through to Hudson confirmed that this was no enemy – quite the opposite – an ally.

But who . . .?

Hudson really didn't have a clue!

The face faded and disappeared and Hudson found

himself looking at his own reflection again – wondering if it had all been some sort of dream.

A short while later, the train arrived at Oxford Central and pulled into the station. Striker and Molly stirred and yawned.

'Oh dear, Hudson,' Molly said as she stretched and turned to face him, 'you look like you've seen a ghost.'

Hudson took the blue rucksack down from the rack above his head and looked back at her with a forced smile. 'Molly – you don't know the half of it . . . while you and Striker were asleep I saw *two* ghosts!'

It was only as they were getting off the train that Hudson realised that nobody had been to ask for their tickets or 'zone passes'. Nobody had got on or off the train. And now, looking over the empty platform at just after midnight, it was as if he and Molly and the dog were the only creatures alive on the planet.

'Come on,' he said to Molly, trying to sound encouraging. 'I think there may be somebody waiting to meet us. Hopefully, he's going to be a help. With a bit of luck we could be back in Danvers Green by late this afternoon.'

Hudson saw by Molly's face that the prospect of being home so soon cheered her up. 'Have we got enough money for a hotel?' she asked pleadingly. 'I'd kill for a bath right now . . . and some hot food and . . .'

A tall shape suddenly loomed out of the shadows by the side of the station exit. Striker rushed forward a few metres, growled and stood protectively in front of his two friends.

A clear, polite voice rang out from the darkness: 'Over here, you two . . . and don't worry. There's a bath and hot food at my place. Come on . . . follow me . . . we need to move!'

The figure moved closer, and as the station lights illuminated the face, they saw the cheerful smile. Hudson recognised it immediately. Molly grabbed his arm.

'Who is he, Hudson? Is he the one you said would be waiting?'

'Yes, and you can trust him, Moll,' Hudson reassured her. 'He's one of the "ghosts" I told you about . . . the friendly one.'

'Hi . . . the name's Bikramjit Oberai – but you can call me Bikram. This is all so exciting! I've got bikes. I hope you can both ride.'

Molly hesitated and then joined Hudson in trotting after the friendly figure, affirming at the same time that they could both ride bicycles.

Within minutes, Bikram was leading the two friends through a deserted town centre and onwards into the shadows of darkened lonely streets enclosed by the ancient buildings of Oxford University.

Some time later a sign on an ivy-covered wall appeared before them: ALL HALLOWS COLLEGE

'We're nearly there,' Bikram whispered. 'Keep as quiet as you can. There are alarms everywhere. And try to keep the dog quiet . . . they're not allowed in college. Unfortunately, despite modern technology, some traditions still survive and we have a college porter to watch over us.'

They swung into a little entrance and watched as Bikram placed the palm of his hand over a small rectangular panel at the side of an arched wooden door. A whirring sound heralded the opening of the door and they followed Bikram through, parking their cycles in a covered shelter just inside the entrance.

Striker sniffed around the dewy ground as Hudson and Molly tried to make out their unfamiliar surroundings.

Bikram led them to the far corner of a quadrangle, through a doorway and up a spiral staircase. At the top of the stairs they reached a corridor with a black and white chequered tiled floor. At the far end of the corridor, Bikram stopped by another door and took a key from the pocket of his denim jacket.

'We're here at last,' he whispered, his eyes sparkling in the half-light. 'Please come inside and make yourselves comfortable.'

Bikram moved through the door and flicked on the light switch. Hudson and Molly followed – they gasped at the sight that greeted them.

'Wow, this is fantastic!' Hudson said as he stared around at the oriental decor.

'I am so glad you like it,' Bikram grinned.

The walls were covered in vibrant colourful drapes, many showing scenes depicting processions of Indian people, elephants and tigers. There was little furniture – the entire floor was covered in brightly patterned carpets and rugs, with more large scatter cushions than Hudson had ever seen.

As Hudson and Molly flopped on to the floor, Striker sniffed around the room, his tail wagging incessantly. Bikram rubbed his hands together and spoke enthusiastically as he stood before them. 'If you two don't mind, I'll light a few candles and put on some soothing music. It's the old-fashioned way but still very effective. It will help us all to relax . . . to chill out.'

Hudson and Molly looked across at each other and smiled.

'Make yourselves at home, both of you, and Molly . . . you can take that bath whenever you're ready.'

'Thanks, Bikram. I might just do that later, but right now I'm just happy to crash out. I feel shattered.'

Hudson watched as Bikram lit several of the many candles placed around the room.

In addition to his black turban, Bikram wore a faded denim jacket over a long shirt and baggy trousers, which looked Indian in origin. He also wore a pair of sporty-looking trainers and Hudson decided that Bikram's mixture of cultural and western clothes gave him an overall 'cool' appearance. The only real evidence of a twenty-year leap in time was the metal band around Bikram's left wrist. It was identical to those they'd seen earlier and it was obviously some sort of communication device.

'So his was the face you saw in the train window, Hudson?' Molly asked, as Bikram walked out and began clattering around in the kitchen.

'Yes, I'm confident he's one of the good guys.'

'Me too,' Molly added. 'I feel as if I've always known him.'

Hudson stretched out across some scatter cushions, leaned his head on one hand and stroked Striker with the other, and at the same time described to Molly in detail the bizarre happenings on the train while she'd been asleep.

A few minutes later, Bikram returned with a tray containing three mugs of herbal tea, a plate of chocolate digestive biscuits and a bowl of water for Striker.

'Wow, yummy,' Molly and Hudson said together as the biscuits were offered around.

'It should keep you going for now,' Bikram smiled. 'We'll have a good breakfast in the morning. We're all going to need lots of energy.'

Hudson and Molly tucked in and managed to forget their worries for a moment – especially when Bikram made Striker sit up on his back legs and beg for a biscuit.

But as the candles burned on and the room filled with the fragrance of incense, it was time for serious talking. Somewhere in the background the gentle sounds of Indian music droned on as Bikram sat cross-legged and began explaining his intervention in their adventure.

'I'm of the Sikh religion and I have a great thirst for learning and knowledge,' he began. 'I also like to meditate and during such times I have often seen your face, Hudson,' Bikram said, his smile looking forced for the first time.

'How much do you know about us?' Molly asked, lying back with her hands behind her head.

'Well, I know about the creature that's after you and I don't think that anyone would envy you in that respect. Your enemy is very bad news!' Bikram answered.

'Can you help us?' Hudson asked directly.

'I'll do my very best. I don't have your powers, Hudson, but I can help you on your way. I know that you're trying to get home.'

'So how much do you know about Mokee Joe?' Molly asked.

'I saw him in Hudson's mind – during your journey on the train. He's a fearful demon. It is a fact that Hudson is going to need all his strength and courage to come out on top.'

'Hudson has both of those . . .' Molly interrupted defensively.

'You're right, Molly,' Bikram replied more encouragingly. 'I've seen the intense power in his mind.'

Hudson started to flush with embarrassment and quickly changed the subject. 'And what about you?' he asked, sitting up and drawing himself into the same cross-legged position. 'How come you can read minds? Are you a transcendent?'

'Hudson – I'm impressed. I wasn't sure you'd know about terms like that. I am only level 2, but by the end of my term here I hope to progress to level 3.'

'What are you studying?'

'Religious Philosophy integrated with Cultural Studies. I'm in my final year. After my exams I'm hoping to go to India to carry out some spiritual research of my own. And you'll be home soon, if things go well. At least "home" on this planet!'

Hudson stared into the dark, clear eyes and permanent smile of his new friend. He seemed to know so much about their situation . . . and he sensed again Bikram's genuine friendliness and willingness to be involved in helping them.

'We're heading for a small town called Danvers Green. Have you heard of it?'

Molly sat up expectantly and waited for Bikram's reply.

'Only since I saw it in your mind. I think it's somewhere in the North Western Zone. I'll see what I can do to get you there. But right now you two need to rest.'

Molly looked across at Hudson and smiled.

'I'll take that bath now, if you don't mind, Bikram,' she said, looking a little more relaxed.

'Help yourself, Molly, there's lots of hot water and clean towels.'

'Thanks,' Molly said as she walked past, stretching her arms. 'Shan't be long, Hudson.'

'Take as long as you like,' Hudson said, looking across at Bikram. 'We'll just carry on chatting for a while longer.'

With Striker curled up in a corner fast asleep, Bikram put out all the candles apart from one, and moved it so that it was directly between Hudson and himself. And then he turned up the music so that the sound of the sitar and the tabla filled their ears.

Finally, as Hudson and Bikram sat cross-legged opposite each other, they began to concentrate hard on the candle flame and prepared to make the trip that they both knew was necessary in order to gauge the next move in Hudson's seemingly eternal battle.

10

THE DREAMING SPIRES

As the pulsating mystical music filled his ears, and the strong smell of incense heightened his sense of relaxation, Hudson watched Bikram's 'other self' rise up in front of him. It seemed the most natural thing in the world and a moment later Hudson was rising up in the same way.

The two entities drifted upwards leaving their material beings sitting cross-legged below, and then they were outside the building, hovering above the rooftops, looking down on the immaculate quadrangle of the college gardens. Seconds later, Hudson found himself chasing his new friend along dimly lit cobbled streets bordered with ivy-clad, high stone college walls.

Together, they glided over cloistered courtyards and

soared over rooftops; they dodged around ancient spires and Hudson stared down curiously at the fearsome stone gargoyles. They swooped along deserted streets, floated past world-famous libraries and drifted by impressive art galleries. They followed the course of the river as it passed through some of the most majestically landscaped grounds that Hudson had ever seen. They fleetingly visited all of the university's celebrated colleges.

The beauty of the night-time scenery was breathtaking and, just for the moment, Hudson forgot about his nightmare situation; he began to feel good about himself and optimistic about the future.

Bikram sensed Hudson's jubilation and reminded him of why they were really there.

Hudson nodded in agreement and joined his nocturnal companion in soaring at great speed upward towards the stars. On reaching the top of their amazing ascent Hudson looked over to Orion and sighed inwardly.

And then he looked down.

A myriad of twinkling lights shone beneath them, complementing the starry sky above. Hudson and Bikram hovered there and concentrated on what they were looking for.

Bikram closed his eyes for several minutes, opened them again and shrugged his shoulders. 'He's out of my range – I can't locate him,' he communicated.

But Hudson's mental powers were superior to those of his friend. He closed his eyes in a similar way and a few seconds later pointed away in a southerly direction and beckoned Bikram to follow.

The two of them dropped at terrific speed, all the time scanning below, until Hudson saw what he was looking for – down towards ground level – a cluster of thin, blue, parallel lines glowing conspicuously from within the darkness of the countryside.

Hudson saw the puzzled look on Bikram's face and beckoned him to drop. As they descended further the incredible scene made itself clear to them.

A long line of electricity pylons bordered the fields alongside the inky water of the Oxford canal. A solitary narrow boat made its way slowly and purposefully beside them. Both Hudson and Bikram knew at once who was steering it.

It was Mokee Joe.

As the demon travelled northwards towards the city, he was locked on to the power in the cables – they crackled and hissed and glowed blue as he absorbed their charge into his hungry circuits.

Bikram wanted to drop lower and take a closer look, but Hudson stopped him. He knew that Mokee Joe was also capable of leaving his physical self and might decide to join them!

No . . . it was enough for now to know his enemy's position.

He studied the scene and calculated with incredible speed and accuracy that if the boat continued at its present rate of knots it wouldn't reach Oxford until first light. And that wasn't allowing for the seven locks that needed negotiating. But in any case, Hudson predicted that Mokee Joe would probably desert the boat before reaching the city in order to keep out of sight. All in all, Hudson reckoned they had about five hours before his enemy was back within striking distance.

Like two flying phantoms, Hudson and Bikram sped back towards the distant spires and headed for All Hallows College.

With the throbbing rhythm of the sitar and tabla still resonating somewhere in their subconscious, the two allies dropped down towards the corner of the quadrangle and allowed themselves to pass through the lichen-covered tiles of the college roof . . . down through the attic, full of students' suitcases, and . . . Hudson stopped himself as he saw the top of Molly's head.

She was relaxing in the bath and casually playing with a large, yellow plastic duck on the surface of the bubbly foam.

Hudson giggled inwardly, drifted back up through the ceiling, found his way into the next room, and dropped down into his body, which was still sitting cross-legged on the cushion where he'd left it.

And then he was his physical self again, looking straight into Bikram's smiling face.

The two friends reached over and shook each other's hands in mutual respect of their mental achievement. It had been a night that the two of them would remember for ever.

A few minutes later, the bathroom door opened and Molly appeared wearing a bathrobe that was too big for her. She had a towel wrapped around her head like a turban and this greatly amused Bikram.

'Have you guys been sitting there all this time?' she said nonchalantly. 'It beats me what you find to talk about.'

'And I don't know how you can lie in the bath all that time,'

Hudson teased back. 'I bet you've been playing with Bikram's yellow plastic duck.'

Molly tilted her head on one side, removed her 'turban' and started drying her hair. She gave Hudson an intense look. 'How did you know that . . .'

Hudson looked across at Bikram and winked. 'All students have a yellow plastic duck, don't they, Bikram? It helps remind them of home when they feel a bit homesick.'

'Absolutely right, Hudson.' Bikram winked back. 'Back in Croydon, we had five ducks, one for each of my four brothers and myself. And they all had names – mine was called Quackers.'

And before Molly could say anything else, the two spiritual companions broke into uncontrollable laughter.

Hudson picked Striker up underneath his arm and sneaked him down into the courtyard for a final chance to do what dogs need to do before they turn in for the night – or at least what was left of it. A few minutes later he returned and found Molly flopped on a large cushion flicking through a book on yoga. Bikram was in the kitchen tidying up and preparing a few things for the morning. As Striker settled himself down Hudson gave Molly a complete update of his out-of-body adventure and finished by saying: '. . . so we've around four or five hours at the most before Mokee Joe catches up with us. It's two thirty in the morning now so we should be able to sleep for a few hours and then we'll have to be up and away.'

They chatted some more over a hot milky drink that Bikram had prepared – and then they finally turned in.

Hudson, Bikram and Striker found cushions and spread themselves out in the sitting room. Molly was offered Bikram's bed in the one other room and she accepted.

And so it was that just after three in the morning, one student of philosophy, one alien adventurer, one very clean but slightly bemused young girl and one plucky Jack Russell terrier settled down and began to sleep the sleep of the dead. The room was awash with the sound of rasping, snoring and grunting – even from Molly's bedroom. Everyone dreamed on – all problems momentarily forgotten.

It was such a pity that no one had given a thought to setting an alarm.

11

$$\frac{\Delta f}{\Delta f^a} = \frac{dt}{dS} - \emptyset + \sqrt{e}$$

$$E = MC^2 \qquad S = ut + \frac{1}{2}at^2$$

A Brief Lesson in Time

Hudson was the first to awake – for three reasons . . .

The first was that somewhere in the distance he could hear a police siren. The second was the familiar dull throbbing headache and the third was that Striker was licking his face and panting enthusiastically in his ear.

He sat up quickly and rooted around under one of the cushions for the pocket watch. His brain went into panic mode as he read the time . . . 9.30 am!

'Good boy, Striker! Good boy!' Hudson patted the little terrier and looked around the room. Bikram was curled up asleep on some cushions over in one corner. The door of the bedroom where Molly was sleeping was closed, gentle snoring sounding from the other side.

Hudson rushed over and roused Bikram and then knocked loudly on the bedroom door.

Within fifteen minutes, everyone was up, dressed and rushing a hastily prepared breakfast of tea, toast and cereal – Bikram said that they should take on as much carbohydrate as they could – they needed energy just as much as Mokee Joe!

'I'm so sorry, Hudson,' Bikram said. 'I think that our nocturnal expedition must have taken it out of us.'

'I'm not really surprised,' Hudson replied. 'The last time I made a trip like that I slept for three days.'

'It's true,' Molly confirmed. 'I visited him in hospital. We all thought he was dying.'

Another police siren sounded in the distance and Hudson frowned as he bit into a piece of toast. 'I'm getting a bad feeling.'

Bikram took a sip of tea and looked at him. 'Yes, I think I can sense trouble too. I think this sleepy university town is awakening to your problem. Someone may well be on to you.'

'Who do you mean?' Molly asked, feeding Striker a piece of toast.

Hudson stood up and dusted the crumbs off his clothes. 'It's anybody's guess! The authorities, the police, Mokee Joe . . . they're all after us. Remember what the sea-witch said? We need to keep at least one step ahead of everyone. I think this oversleeping business has put us more like a step back. They're almost on us . . . all of them!'

Molly sighed and put her empty plate down.

'He's right,' Bikram went on. 'You and Hudson are being closed in on. We need to get you on your way. I've got an idea. Just give me a few minutes.' Hudson looked at Molly as Bikram went out of the room.

'You really believe Mokee Joe is close?' Molly asked nervously.

Hudson walked over to one of the leaded arched windows at the side of the room and looked out across the lawned gardens. He quickly turned back and answered Molly's question: 'He could be very close. There are a couple of policemen over at the main entrance talking to a man wearing a suit and a bowler hat.'

Bikram walked back in the room, at the same time adjusting his metal wristband. 'That's Jollop, the college porter,' he stated, his eyes wide with concern. 'We really do need to move quickly.'

Hudson and Molly watched with fascination as Bikram spoke into his wristband and arranged transport for the next stage of their journey home. It seemed a friend of his had organised a theatre trip from a nearby college and the coach would be heading roughly in the direction of Danvers Green. It was due to leave Oxford at two o'clock and there were spare seats – they could even travel free – as a favour to Bikram.

'So we just need to keep our heads down and stay low until then,' Hudson said.

'And that will be easier in the city centre,' Bikram added.

'Could we get rid of these stupid school uniforms?' Molly asked, glowering down at her blue tracksuit.

'That will not be a problem,' Bikram answered, adjusting his turban. 'I know where all the best donor shops are – it'll give us something to do.'

Molly gave Hudson a puzzled look as they prepared to move on.

'Do you think he means "charity shops"?' Hudson whispered to her as they sneaked out of the room and down the chequered corridor.

Molly nodded thoughtfully.

They passed only one student on their way out of the building, a man dressed in heavy cord trousers and a baggy checked shirt. He was standing at the end of the corridor staring at something in his hand. He only looked up at the last second.

'Hi, Bikram. Friends of yours?'

'Yes – they're cousins – down for the day.'

'Oh, fine. Hi.' He smiled at Hudson and Molly and then looked back to the small panel. 'What do you reckon to this?'

He held up the miniature television screen to show the three friends. It seemed to be some sort of electronic newspaper and Hudson gulped as he saw the headline: 'MADMAN CAUSES CHAOS ON LONDON UNDER-GROUND'.

They feigned their surprise, made their excuses and moved on with renewed urgency. A few seconds later, they were down the stone staircase and out in the fresh air. They looked over to the porter's lodge and were relieved to see that the policeman had moved on and the college porter was standing on his own.

After a quick discussion, Bikram went over and talked to Jollop and distracted him whilst Hudson, Molly and Striker sneaked over and waited by the same arched door they'd entered the previous evening.

Striker was desperate to stake his newfound territory and Molly had to drag him away and discourage him from watering all the bicycles.

A few minutes later, Bikram reappeared and opened the electronically operated door.

Outside the college, moving swiftly down a cobbled street lined with lime trees, they became aware of a number of policemen standing around, many talking into various small devices, and seemingly on the lookout.

Hudson and Molly couldn't help feeling conspicuous wearing their school uniforms – people would wonder why they were not at school and hanging around with an undergraduate – the sooner they got rid of them the better.

They began a tour of donor shops and Hudson had guessed right – they were just charity shops.

By noon, Hudson and Molly were kitted out in different clothes.

Molly was now feeling much more comfortable in a pair of purple cord jeans and old roll-neck white sweater and some sort of blue, plastic waterproof with a hood. The clothes were well worn, but they were clean and smelt fresh.

Hudson had gone for a black open-necked shirt over a black T-shirt. He'd even found a pair of black fingerless gloves, which he'd taken a special liking to. Tight black jeans and a pair of old trainers completed his 'new wardrobe'.

'You look really cool in black, Hudson,' Molly said admiringly.

'Pure Gothic,' Bikram added, almost laughing out loud.

Over a light lunch, Bikram explained that the word 'fashion' had all but disappeared from the English language.

Now everyone wore whatever he or she felt most comfortable in. Most students of foreign origin, like Bikram, liked to associate themselves with their culture, but the old styles of the pre and post millennium decades were just as popular as ever. The only people who dressed for the occasion these days were older people or the city executives in their dark flannel suits.

After lunch, Hudson complained of headaches and this made him extremely nervous. The prospect of walking around the streets and killing time until two o'clock suddenly seemed hazardous.

'Look!' Hudson shouted, pointing towards an arched entrance.

Striker barked enthusiastically as Bikram and Molly read the sign:

Today
THE STOKEHAM LECTURE
Professor W. R. Stokeham BSc MPhil MRIAP
Institute of Astronomical Physics
11.30–2.00 pm

'That's the guy the sea-witch told you to look out for, isn't it, Hudson?' Molly gasped.

Hudson spotted a policeman standing across the other side of the road eyeing them suspiciously. As their gazes met, the policeman began speaking into his wristband.

'It is,' Hudson replied, 'and now might be a good time to go in there and take a look. We've still got some time, haven't we, Bikram?'

'Just a little,' Bikram replied, leading them through the archway, 'the bus leaves from a place not too far from here. Follow me. I know this lecture theatre quite well.'

Hudson picked Striker up and followed Molly and Bikram through the arched entrance. Taking a fleeting glance over his shoulder he saw that the policeman was already crossing the road towards them.

A moment later they were through another door and treading stealthily up a creaking flight of wooden stairs. The walls were oak-panelled and smelt strongly of polish. As they crept on along a gloomy corridor, a man's deep voice echoed in the distance and grew louder with every step.

'Have you come across this Professor Stokeham before?' Hudson whispered to Bikram as they reached an open door at the top of the stairs.

'Oh yes. Just about everyone in Oxford knows him. He's quite famous in intellectual and scientific circles. He and his team of physicists have recently discovered the "Ribbon Loop Theory" of time and space.'

Before Hudson had chance to question Bikram further, they passed through the open doorway and found themselves on the top row of an impressive lecture theatre. Only two other students were seated towards the middle of the row, both totally engrossed in the scene down below . . . and what a scene!

Hudson's eyes almost popped out as he peered down over the steeply descending rows of what looked like ancient choir stalls. Down at the bottom of the theatre a large man wearing a grey suit, complete with bow tie and thick spectacles, was standing behind a huge wooden bench and pointing at an impressive screen filled with all kinds of mathematical symbols and formulae.

In between Hudson and the professor, the rows of seats were jam-packed with students, all with laptops, all punching away frantically on their keypads.

Striker let out a little whine.

'Sshhh . . .' Hudson said, placing him gently down on to the floor. But nobody heard. It seemed everyone was totally absorbed in what the man was saying.

'That must be Professor Stokeham?' Molly whispered, pointing down to the thick head of white hair.

'Yes . . . that's him,' Bikram whispered back. 'He recently won the Nobel Prize for pursuing and developing the early theories of the great scientists of the millennium . . . Kestraling and Rider, for example. Some of my colleagues back at All Hallows told me that the professor and his team are on the verge of a major breakthrough – they are close to understanding the total concept of time and space.'

Molly listened to Bikram with fascination, but Hudson heard nothing. He was too busy studying the mass of symbols on the big screen and deciphering the complex mathematical formulae at speed in his computer-like brain.

'Hudson has gone very quiet,' Bikram whispered to Molly.

'I think he's trying to understand the professor's work – that jumble on the screen. He's into all that sort of thing,' Molly replied softly.

Professor Stokeham suddenly looked up and began his summary: 'And so in conclusion, ladies and gentlemen, I say to you that if we can build on this complex equation' – he pointed to the lowest row of symbols on the screen – 'then we should soon have the solution that has evaded us for so long.'

The professor put down his metal pointing stick on the bench, folded his arms and looked up at the sea of faces peering over their laptops. 'And now if there are any questions . . .'

Before anyone could say anything, Striker let out a loud bark and turned back towards the open door growling fiercely.

'What's going on?' the professor shouted up at them. 'And what are those young people doing up there?'

Hudson shouted back down at him, 'You've made a simple mistake.'

Every face in the lecture theatre turned and looked up at the boy with the strange hairstyle.

Before anyone could say anything, Hudson advanced down the narrow flight of steps in the middle of the auditorium. 'That letter "e" in the bottom line . . . does it have a value of 2.718 . . .?'

'Yes, of course,' the professor interrupted impatiently.

A general hubbub sounded from the audience. Many of the students started laughing, convinced the scene developing in front of them was some sort of wind-up. The professor seemed to be of the same opinion, but he was far from amused. 'Would someone please remove . . .'

Hudson reached the bottom step and now it was his turn to interrupt. 'That "e", the constant, it should be squared, and that decimal value you have further back in the calculation, 0.35 recurring, it should in fact be 0.3556. With these values you should find that the earlier wave equations all key in and the whole thing balances . . .'

A loud roar of laughter rippled around the audience.

Meanwhile, Striker began barking continuously from the back and everyone turned their heads and looked up again.

'Hudson!' Molly shouted frantically. 'We need to get out of here.'

'Molly's right,' Bikram shouted, for the first time not smiling.

But Hudson was absorbed in looking at the professor, standing there, hands on hips, studying the mass of equations. The professor turned to a laptop on his desk and started punching away on the keys. And then the big man looked up and Hudson saw the revelation in his face as his expression changed from frowning irritation into a beaming smile.

The audience went very quiet and stared at the professor in disbelief as he spoke again. 'My God, I don't know who you are, young fellow, or where you've come from, but what you've just said makes absolute sense. In fact . . .' But that was all the dumbfounded lecturer had time to say.

If Hudson had just shown his true academic potential, he had also shown his lack of experience in allowing himself to be distracted again. His mind was full of mathematical symbols and numbers, but a sharp pain in his temples suddenly reminded him of the real reason he was there.

And that's when Molly's voice shrieked out the dreaded words: 'HE'S HERE, HUDSON! MOKEE JOE! HE'S HERE!'

12

Battle of Wits

If Hudson had been distracted, Striker certainly hadn't. He'd tried to bark his warning, but now it was too late. The terrifying figure of Mokee Joe rushed through the top doorway, and as Bikram, Molly and Striker edged backwards, Hudson, the professor and the sea of students turned and saw him standing there, glowering from the top row of the auditorium.

The Mokee Man presented an awesome sight.

First the fire, and then the clash with Malcolm's van followed by his big fall down the steps in Paddington Station, had all combined to make the sinister figure even more horrific in its appearance.

The long coat looked revolting – blackened and torn and

stinking of oil. The crumpled black hat was torn in several places and beneath it the hideous face looked even more fearsome than Hudson remembered. Now it was lopsided, one demonic scowling eye set higher in the cracked, orangey-grey flesh than the other. The long bony hands, charred and distorted, reached out from the ends of the ragged coat sleeves.

But the strength and purpose were still there.

As Striker ran down the central aisle with Molly and Bikram following, Mokee Joe's heavy boots thudded into the ancient wooden floorboards as he charged in their wake.

The lecture theatre immediately turned into a scene of chaos.

Whilst half of the audience stood and screamed for fear of their lives, the rest of the students just laughed and remained seated, still convinced that the whole thing was some sort of joke.

Hudson reacted at lightning speed.

All in a split second he reached over to the huge bench, snatched up the professor's metal pointing stick, and with enormous strength and accuracy, threw it like a miniature javelin towards his advancing enemy.

It struck Mokee Joe in the neck, entering one side and sticking out the other. The effect was to stop the monster dead in its tracks half way down the steps. Those still watching gasped in shock as the tall, gangly figure began to surge with blue, crackling electricity. The metal stick glowed and hissed, but Mokee Joe calmly withdrew it and in a show of strength, he snapped it in two like a dry twig before continuing his downward charge towards Hudson.

Those who had thought the whole thing a joke now changed their minds. Abandoned laptops crashed to the ground as their owners clambered over the ancient stalls and bolted towards the exit doors. Screams rang out everywhere as panic and pandemonium took over – especially when both lower exits became blocked with bodies trying to get out.

Only Hudson and the professor stood their ground.

'WHAT ON EARTH IS GOING ON HERE?' Professor Stokeham ranted from behind his bench.

Meanwhile, with about a dozen steps still to go, Mokee Joe made a tremendous leap and landed his huge boots firmly on the professor's work surface. With a nerve-wracking electronic scream he waved his fists in the air and towered over Hudson and the retreating crowd of students.

Molly, Bikram and Striker found themselves by the side of the professor's bench, almost within reach of Hudson, but then they couldn't move – there were too many students crushing in on them. Molly stared up at the horrendous figure in time to see the long, lethal fingers pointing down towards Hudson's head.

'WE'VE GOT TO DO SOMETHING!' Molly screamed.

As quick as a flash Bikram pulled the turban off his head, tore at the silk material from where it was pinned and placed one end in Striker's mouth.

'Good boy! You know what you have to do . . .'

He manhandled the little dog through the crowd on to the bench and Striker needed no telling what to do next. The clever animal weaved his way in and out of Mokee Joe's huge ankles taking the length of silk from Bikram's turban with him.

As the fearsome monster finally unleashed the inevitable electric charge, Hudson dived to one side. The professor, meanwhile, who'd seen everything, read Bikram's actions and lunged forward, pushing with all his strength on the huge frame standing on the bench in front of him.

Striker had worked well and had distributed the entire length of Bikram's turban around Mokee Joe's feet.

'GET OUT OF THE WAY,' Bikram yelled to no one in particular. 'THE ENEMY IS ABOUT TO FALL!'

Mokee Joe found himself in no position to disagree.

Totally oblivious to what had been going on in his ankle region, the professor's shove sent him off balance so that he began to topple backwards. More electricity shot out from his fingers, but this time it angled up towards the ceiling and struck a large fluorescent tube. The glass shattered and rained down with dramatic effect. Finally, the monster's huge frame crashed back on to the edge of the bench and he rolled helplessly on to the floor.

'FAR STEPS UP TO THE EXIT!' Hudson yelled to his friends.

Most of the shocked audience had got out by this time and Bikram and Molly followed his instructions without difficulty. The professor decided to join in with their exodus.

Meanwhile, Mokee Joe rolled about on the floor, his feet still bound in the confusing tangle of Bikram's turban.

The escape party raced through the top door and no one spoke as they leapt down the old wooden stairway, three steps at a time. No one even bothered speaking to the policeman sitting on the bottom step looking dazed and bewildered. Hudson recognised him as the policeman who'd followed them across the road earlier.

Once outside in the fresh air, they found themselves surrounded by groups of shocked students – it would only be a matter of time before the authorities arrived in force – and Hudson knew they had to get away fast. Even so, he had to speak to the professor.

'Professor Stokeham . . . we were told to look out for you . . . do you know anything about me?'

The professor understandably looked agitated. 'No . . . I don't even know your name. What's all this about and who or what is that thing in there?'

Hudson, Molly and Bikram looked at each other, each wondering what to say next.

As a police car drew up outside the arched entrance, Bikram spoke in an urgent tone of voice: 'Hudson, we need to go. Your coach leaves in five minutes. I am so sorry, Professor. I don't mean to be rude, but now is not the time for explanations.'

Molly grabbed Hudson's arm and pointed up towards the top of the building. Hudson swallowed hard as he saw what she was pointing at. Mokee Joe had somehow got up on to the roof and was peering at them from behind a towering, old chimney stack. Hudson worried that he might try to leap down on them.

Molly echoed his thoughts. 'Let's go, Hudson – he's going to jump!'

Without another word, Hudson pushed his way through the groups of students and followed Bikram towards the entrance. Molly followed carrying Striker in her arms.

'Hey . . . wait!' the professor called after them. 'We need

to talk some more . . .'

But his voice only trailed away into the distance as the foursome raced out of the entrance and off through the crowds of shoppers.

When they reached the college, the bus was already waiting with the engine running. A tall girl carrying a clipboard approached them as they ran towards it.

'Oh, hi, Bikram. So these are your friends? And a dog . . . nobody said anything about a dog!'

'Striker will be fine,' Bikram said, with a half-smile, half-frown on his face. 'He'll probably spend the whole journey asleep under the seat, won't he, Molly?'

'Exactly right! He's no trouble whatsoever – he's a good boy.' Molly nuzzled her face up to Striker and he licked her affectionately.

'I'll have to check with the driver, but it's probably cool.' The girl smiled. 'You'd better get on. Everyone else is on board so we're about ready for the off.'

'It's time to part ways,' Bikram said with genuine sorrow in his voice. 'The coach will drop you at Stratford – you know – Shakespeare country. You'll easily get to Danvers Green from there. It's been brilliant meeting you both. Who knows . . . perhaps we'll meet up again under happier circumstances.'

Hudson took his rucksack off, ready to get on the coach. 'Can we keep in touch?' he said, pointing a finger towards his temple.

'I'm afraid my range is small,' Bikram frowned. 'I've a friend who helps me to calculate my thought transference capability. So far my record is forty kilometres – you'll be travelling well out of my range – about one hundred and fifty K from here.'

Molly waved to Bikram as she carried the little dog up the steps of the coach.

Hudson asked one last question as he followed. 'What do you think *my* range is, Bikram? How far can I send messages from *my* head?'

'I feel certain, Hudson, that one day, you and your people will reach the far ends of the universe . . . you're much more powerful than you realise. Now take care and take this.' He handed Hudson a neatly wrapped rectangular package. 'Don't unwrap it now. Look at it later. It is a gift. It is a tradition that every Sikh should have one for protection. I offer it to you for yours. Take care.'

With a final smile and without another word, Bikram turned and disappeared into the crowd.

Seeing his new friend vanish from sight so quickly made Hudson feel more vulnerable. He shoved the package into his rucksack and made his way to the back seat of the bus. He sat next to Molly and saw that Striker was already curled up at her feet. The girl with the clipboard did a final head count and the doors hissed shut.

As the coach picked its way carefully through the dense traffic, heading for the city outskirts, Hudson looked anxiously out of the rear window. There was no sign of his enemy – yet – but he knew it would only be a matter of time before Mokee Joe was back on the trail.

Hudson sat down and sighed.

'Are you OK?' Molly asked, tugging at his arm affectionately.

'I am, Moll, but for how long? Mokee Joe seems indestructible. He's been set on fire, smashed into by a van, hurtled down station steps, speared through the neck – but he just keeps on coming! What do I have to do?'

Molly looked at him sympathetically and tugged his sleeve again.

'You're succeeding, Hudson. You've done everything GA told you to do. You're leading him back to Danvers Green, and so far, he's not been caught by the police or blown anybody up and we're still going strong. I just know that when we get home things will work out – I'm sure they will!'

Before long, as the coach sped out into the surrounding countryside, Hudson suddenly remembered Bikram's gift.

He took the rectangular package from his bag and carefully unwrapped it. Inside the neat packaging, Hudson found a white, rectangular box and he gasped as he opened it. It contained a long, lethal-looking knife with a jewelled handle. And then Hudson remembered that Bikram had said something about 'protection'.

He quickly rewrapped it and put it carefully back inside his bag.

Right now Hudson needed all the protection he could get and he just knew that somehow this knife was going to play an important part in his continuing battle with Mokee Joe!

13

Ups and DOWNS

Hudson looked out of the coach window and saw that they were crawling alongside what looked like a small airfield. Groups of people wearing strange suits were standing around surrounded by even stranger-looking machines.

'It's a Commuter Flying Point,' the girl with the clipboard said as she walked up and sat in a spare seat just in front of Hudson. 'Have you not seen one before?'

'No . . . what's a Commuter Flying Point?' Hudson asked, still staring out of the window.

'Those machines are commuter microlights – they're very sophisticated. Business executives use them to commute from one place to another. I can't believe you've never seen one before – you often see them flying overhead. Where did Bikram say you came from?'

'Danvers Green. Do they fly at night?'

'Not very often . . . except around London. It's the quickest form of transport these days – if you can afford it.'

So that explains the strange lights in the sky at Piccadilly Circus, Hudson thought to himself.

He looked back into the field and watched with fascination as a pilot dressed in some sort of white boiler suit strapped himself into one of the machines and took off into the sky. The one-man plane soared off at a tremendous speed. It had a curved windscreen and Hudson guessed that the pilot would need it to protect himself from the wind speed.

Several more microlights swooped in and made impressive landings and then Hudson wasn't able to see any more as the coach moved on and the amazing scene was left behind.

The bus managed to pick up a little more speed as it trundled on along the busy A40 until, eventually, it reached the motorway. Hudson watched with interest as the coach turned down a slip road and finally drew up at some sort of pay kiosk. The driver handed over some money and, after being given what looked like a plastic card, pulled away and filtered the coach into the second lane of an impressive six-lane carriageway. A sign told Hudson that they had joined the M40.

Like the M20 up to London, the motorway heaved with traffic, and only the most streamlined cars moved at any real speed in the outermost lanes.

Molly was dozing gently as Hudson dug an elbow into her arm. 'Hey, Molly! Get a load of this!'

Molly groaned, stretched and looked over Hudson's shoulder through the coach window. A huge black limousine had appeared in the outermost lane and was cruising in line with them.

'Wow . . . that's some stretch limo,' Molly gasped. '*And it's got no wheels!*'

'It seems to be riding on air,' Hudson gasped. 'It's the first time I've seen anything in lane six . . . it must be somebody pretty special,' he added. 'Look! It's keeping level with us.'

'It's a bit spooky,' Molly said, leaning further over to the window. 'It's like they're watching us, but we can't see them.'

Hudson nodded in agreement. The windows were all blacked out. It was impossible to see the occupants, and judging by the length of the car there could have been any number of them inside. But before there was time to make any more comments, the impressive limousine accelerated at a breathtaking rate and disappeared into the distance.

'Blast! I didn't even have time to read the number plates . . . it moved off too fast,' Hudson complained.

'Hudson, do you think we're nearly there?' Molly changed the subject. 'I really could do with a loo stop and I think Striker might need some water, he's starting to pant quite a lot.'

Hudson stared down at the Jack Russell curled up by Molly's feet. The dog looked back at him with soulful eyes, as if to say, 'She's right – I am ready for a drink.'

Hudson made his way to the front of the bus, had a quick word with the girl with the clipboard and returned to his seat. 'It's OK, Moll. We're pulling up at the next motorway services – in about ten minutes.'

Molly smiled and nodded and Striker gave a soft little bark of approval. 'Do you know, Hudson . . . I swear that dog understands every word we say . . . it's uncanny.'

'You're right,' Hudson replied. 'No wonder the sea-witch called him Smarty. He's smarter than anyone realises. I can't help feeling he's a part of all this – as if he was meant to be here all along.'

Striker barked, as if in agreement, and Hudson and Molly looked down at him and laughed.

Ten minutes later, as promised, the coach moved over towards a slip road leading into the much-awaited motorway services. As they pulled in, Hudson noticed that the driver was talking into something on the dashboard. He manoeuvred the coach into a parking bay, switched off the engine and leaned over and spoke to the young woman with the clipboard.

Hudson sensed immediately that something was wrong.

'OK folks,' the girl in charge shouted down the coach. 'We're stopping here for about twenty minutes. Please don't be late back on board. Could the children at the back please remain seated until everyone else is off the coach.'

'Hudson, what's going on?' Molly nudged him as she spoke. 'Something's wrong, isn't it?'

Hudson got up and looked out of the coach window. Other coaches lined up beside them and crowds of people were coming and going towards the main service area. In the distance, lines of cars in the main car park were also intermingled with their occupants moving in and out of them . . . and then Hudson's heart skipped a beat. He was just able to make out the top of an enormously long black limousine threading its way through the car park towards them. A few seconds later, it emerged from the sea of cars and entered into the coach park and drew up beside them.

Now, Hudson was able to read the number plate easily.

GSU I

'I should have known,' Hudson gasped. 'It's the authorities. They've caught up with us.'

The girl with the clipboard walked down the aisle towards them. Hudson noticed that she looked very tense, her normally relaxed smile turned into a serious frown. 'There's some people would like a word with you. Will you come with me, please?'

Hudson looked at Molly and nodded.

The girl led them down the steps of the bus and over towards the waiting car. Even close up, it was still impossible to see inside, and, as yet, the doors had remained firmly closed.

As the girl ushered them closer, Striker gave a little growl and Molly picked him up and held him close. Suddenly, a door about half way down the length of the car glided silently open and a voice from inside ordered them calmly but firmly to get inside.

Without hesitation, Hudson moved forward and climbed in. Molly followed, still clutching Striker.

The door slid shut again and Hudson and Molly marvelled at their surroundings.

There were five occupants in the car – the driver and someone in the front passenger seat, both with backs towards them, and three people all clicking away on computers spread out along the far side of the car and facing away from them. Wires snaked out from the hardware into metal discs stuck on the side of the operatives' heads, giving them a very sinister appearance.

Hudson and Molly sat on a long seat down the nearside of the car and looked nervously around. It seemed that the stretch limo was some sort of mobile computer network.

The two men in the front were dressed in black. The computer operators were dressed in casual clothes – jeans and T-shirts.

'Hudson Brown and Molly Stevens . . . it really is you . . . it's incredible!'

The voice came from the man in the passenger seat, as he turned round to face them. He wore dark glasses and his face was almost set in stone . . . just a glimmer of a smile.

'*The chief man in black!*' Hudson exclaimed loudly. 'I never expected to see you again!'

'The name's Doubleday,' the man in black replied gravely, 'and I can well imagine your surprise.'

'So how much do you know about what's been happening to Molly and me?'

'Everything,' Doubleday said, with just a hint of feeling in his voice. 'Absolutely everything.'

Striker gave a little growl again.

'Would you put the dog outside, please?' It was more an order than a request. 'We really don't need animals in here.'

'Either he stays or we don't,' Molly spoke up defensively.

'She's right,' Hudson chipped in. 'That "dog", as you put it, is a vital member of our team.'

'Very well.' Doubleday's voice softened a little more. 'We'd better get straight down to business. We know about the crash, we know about your uncle's unfortunate end . . .'

'Did you find his body?' Hudson interrupted, his voice trembling a little.

'Yes, don't worry yourself about that. Your uncle's body is safe in a government mortuary. We'll take good care of it.'

'And do you know what GA . . . er . . . I mean my uncle, told us?' Hudson went on.

'Yes – I think so. Mrs Hollingworth is helping us with our enquiries.'

'Who's Mrs Hollingworth?' Molly asked.

'She lives by the sea in Kent and has a son called Malcolm . . . I think you know her as . . .'

'. . . the sea-witch!' Hudson completed the sentence. 'Are they both OK?'

'They're both fine and send their regards,' Doubleday replied, this time smiling more warmly. 'We know all about your proposed journey back home – to Danvers Green – and it may surprise you to know that we're here to help you in your quest. We also know all about Bikram Oberai, who also sends his regards, and we have spoken at length to Professor Stokeham.'

Doubleday paused and then he continued in a much more serious tone of voice. 'It would seem that Oxford is still in a state of panic – the events that unfolded there were dramatic to say the least – as they were in London. The tube stations are only just getting back to normal.'

Hudson noticed that all the time they were being spoken to the men on the computers never looked up. They were totally absorbed in tapping away on the keyboards in front of them.

'And what about Mokee Joe?' Hudson came straight out with it. 'Do you know how dangerous he's become?'

Doubleday stroked his hand back through his head of silvery grey hair. 'Oh yes! The Mokee Man is a living nightmare! Even now the National Grid System is in a complete state of disarray.'

'What's the National Grid System?' Molly asked.

'Basically, it means the electricity supply,' Doubleday explained. 'For some time now, the Mokee Joe creature has been constantly tapping into overhead cables in order to charge himself up and power cuts have resulted all along his trail.'

Suddenly, one of the men on the computers stopped tapping his keys and turned to face him. 'Grid failure at 013 678, sir – about ten miles north-west of Oxford.'

And then another one of the operators, wires trailing from his head, turned and spoke. 'A small CFP within that area is reporting the theft of a SCM Mark3.'

'Damn!' Doubleday whispered audibly.

Hudson's brain worked frantically. CFP . . . Commuter Flying Point. But what's an SCM?

Doubleday answered for him. 'Hudson! It seems that Mokee Joe is back on your trail. He's hijacked a Super Commuter Microlight – one of the most sophisticated and powerful models around. It can travel at high speeds and he'll soon be close on your heels. And, in further response to your first question . . . yes, we do know how dangerous he's become . . . we know all about the quantity of nuclear material that he's carrying around with him.'

'The Triotose!' Hudson added.

'Yes . . . we know that your enemy is carrying a nuclear explosive and that your objective is to lead him back to Danvers Green. God knows how this mess is going to be cleared up, but we have great faith in the knowledge and advice of your uncle – if the solution awaits in Danvers Green then it's our responsibility to get you there as soon as possible.'

'I still don't see why Mokee Joe doesn't just blow himself up and the rest of us with him and be done with it,' Molly stated in a frustrated tone of voice.

It was one of the computer operators who turned and answered Molly's question. 'To trigger the Triotose into a nuclear reaction would require an enormous quantity of electrical charge. It is our opinion that the creature is constantly charging himself from the electricity supply in order to achieve the required threshold level.'

'In any case,' Hudson interrupted, 'he won't risk blowing himself up yet. GA said that as long as he evades capture and believes he has a chance of destroying me he will still follow his survival instincts and keep going.'

'I know,' Doubleday said. 'Your survival is our survival . . . and that's why we all need to work together.'

'Have you been helping us all along?' Molly asked with wide eyes.

'Of course! Without our intervention the police would have picked you up a long time ago . . . and they would no doubt have tried to capture and detain the Mokee Man . . . and then who knows what would have happened?'

The driver spoke quietly into Doubleday's ear so that he continued with a renewed urgency. 'We'd better get you to

Danvers Green. Time is running out and there's more than a few people waiting for your arrival there.'

As the car began to move forwards, Molly almost jumped out of her seat with excitement. 'Our parents?'

'Yes, they will be waiting. They have been preparing for your arrival. But you must realise that your return after twenty years is going to be a big shock for them.'

Hudson watched as Molly nodded solemnly.

'There is also a member of the Stokeham Research Team who is especially keen to meet you. They all await you in the Tennyson Centre, up by your old junior school – Danvers Green Primary.'

Hudson and Molly both swallowed hard.

'So are you driving us there?' Hudson asked.

'Good Lord, no!' Doubleday turned to face the front as the car drew up in a deserted area somewhere around the back of the services. 'The JPHC would take at least an hour to get you there. We have speedier plans.'

'What's a JPHC?' Hudson asked.

'Sorry! Jet Propelled Hover Car . . . that's why it doesn't . . .'

'. . . have any wheels,' Molly finished. 'This is all like science-fiction come to life, Hudson.'

Hudson nodded as Doubleday looked on sympathetically.

The car stopped and Hudson and Molly got out and their eyes opened wide as a bright red helicopter appeared over their heads and descended on to the tarmac in front of them. 'GSU' was painted in bold black letters on the side.

'This should get us there in less than fifteen minutes,' Doubleday said to them.

'I still need the loo,' Molly said nervously, standing cross-legged. 'And Striker needs a drink.'

Doubleday went back into the car and came out with two small capsules. 'Here, take these; there is no time.' He passed Molly one of the capsules and offered Striker the other.

Hudson looked into the eyes of the man. 'Chemicals with opposing effects! The first gets rid of water, the second creates it.'

'Quite right,' Doubleday said, impressed with Hudson's statement. 'Agents use them all the time. And now we must go . . . there is little time to lose. We must get you to Danvers Green ahead of your enemy so that the final encounter can be planned with absolute precision.'

The rotor blades of the helicopter started up and Hudson, Molly (still clutching Striker) and Doubleday ducked down and made their way towards it. Within minutes they were on board and being whisked away up to the heavens.

Peering out of the glass windows, Hudson looked down over the motorway services, growing smaller and more distant by the second. Doubleday nudged him from his seat at the back and passed him a lightweight, all-in-one, zip-up suit and a pack to put on – the same for Molly too. The packs were parachutes and were self-operating. He showed them what to do should any emergency arise – they couldn't afford to take any chances. Molly asked if Striker could have a parachute, but Doubleday just frowned and shook his head.

As the whirlybird soared upwards Hudson noticed a sparkle in Molly's eyes. She had never looked so hopeful since the start of their journey. The helicopter ride was exciting to say the least, and they were heading homewards

– back to their parents – even if they had aged twenty years. And then the men in black – they were pulling out all the stops to help them.

It all evoked such feelings of optimism.

But did it?

Hudson knew that, as yet, the situation was far from resolved. Even if they did make it back home, what could he or anyone else possibly do to get rid of his enemy? After all – *Mokee Joe had become a walking nuclear bomb!*

To add to Hudson's growing pessimism, the weather suddenly changed and huge drops of rain began splattering on to the helicopter's windscreen. As a gust of wind blew them wildly to one side, Molly turned and smiled. Hudson knew it was a forced smile – it was an attempt to reassure him . . . and then he felt intense pain in the sides of his head and watched dumbfounded as her expression changed to shocked horror.

She screamed across at him, '*Hudson . . . what's happening . . . there's blood trickling out of your ears?*'

14

TERRA FIRMA

'It's my head!' Hudson cried out. 'I've got a really sharp pain and it's spreading to my ears.'

Doubleday reached over for the first aid box. 'It's probably got something to do with the air pressure,' he said calmly. 'Do you have any problems with heights?'

'No – I only usually have problems when Mokee Joe is trying to get into my head.'

'But he's not *that* close at the moment, Hudson . . . is he?' Molly asked, holding Striker tighter to her chest as the helicopter wobbled in the storm.

'Well *somebody's* close!' the pilot suddenly chipped in. 'It's one of those SCMs and it's all over the place.' He spoke into a panel on the dashboard and tried to communicate with the erratic pilot. 'Hello . . . are you hearing me . . . are you in difficulty?'

No reply.

'Don't waste your time,' Doubleday said sternly. 'I know only too well who it is – he stole the microlight just a short while ago.'

Hudson pointed over to their left as the fantastic machine came into view. Its wings careered wildly in the strengthening wind and, even as they watched, it swung in perilously close to them.

'It's *him*, isn't it?' Molly asked nervously. Striker sensed her nervousness and licked her face.

Hudson didn't have time to answer.

The microlight loomed closer and everyone saw the demon face grinning from behind the rain-splatted wind-screen. Hudson dabbed the blood from his ears with pads of cotton wool. And then the words formed in his head: *This time you are finished, Tor-3-ergon. I have you at my mercy and now I shall destroy you once and for all.*

They all tensed as Mokee Joe unleashed a bolt of blue lightning from the fingers of his free hand. It struck the rotor blades above their heads and caused the helicopter to rock wildly. 'Oh my God!' the pilot yelled back at them. 'We've been hit . . . the engine's going to stall. Shall I fire back, Sir? I can take him out with a single shot!'

'No! We can't afford the risk. Get ready to eject,' Doubleday ordered in as calm a voice as he could manage. But Hudson sensed the man's panic as he checked the straps of his own parachute before checking Hudson's and Molly's.

The pilot struggled to regain control of the helicopter,

battling against the ferocity of the weather as well as trying to avoid the crazy pilot attacking from their flank. As Molly's face turned a sickly white colour, Hudson tried to reassure her by gripping her arm.

The pilot finally regained some control, but they could only watch helplessly as Mokee Joe swung in again for another strike.

This time the lightning bolt struck the helicopter with such ferocity that the engine stalled completely. Hudson and Molly screamed as the helicopter dropped. Doubleday struggled out of his seat as the pilot tried desperately to control their downward motion.

'We're just going to have to drop under automotive rotation and try to land, Sir – there's no way I can restart the engine.'

As the helicopter levelled a little, Doubleday slid the door of the helicopter back and beckoned to Hudson. 'We might not make it and we can't take any more chances . . . it's time for you to go. Count to three, jump and the parachute will do the rest. Remember what I said about steering it by pulling on the strings. When you get down there, make your way to Danvers Green and find the Tennyson Centre. People will be waiting for you. We're only about twenty or thirty miles off. You'll find your way easily enough – especially a boy with your powers.'

'What about me?' Molly shrieked, her voice full of panic.

'You too, young lady. You follow on. Just count to three and jump. Once you're down, if Hudson doesn't find you, one of my men will. Just get to your destination as soon as you can. But I'm afraid you'll have to leave the dog . . . it's too dangerous . . . he might get in the way of your strings.'

'If I go – he goes!' Molly replied firmly. 'He'll help me when we're down on the ground, won't you, baby?' Striker licked her face and gave a little whimper. Doubleday tutted his disapproval, reached into a storage hold and passed her a small zip-up carry bag. She put Striker inside it so that his head was sticking out and then hung the straps around her neck so that the bag was over her chest. This way, her hands were still free to manage the parachute.

Hudson did the same with his rucksack. 'And what about you and the pilot?' he asked.

'We'll try and dodge Mokee Joe and land as quickly as we can. Once we're on the ground we can get the engine sorted. But we may not make it – which is why you've got to go – *you've got to make it.* Don't worry about us. In any case, once you've bailed out, the Mokee Man will probably leave us alone – after all, it's you he wants.'

'He's bound to come straight after us,' Molly stated, unfastening her seatbelt.

'But he'll have to find somewhere safe to land,' the pilot joined in. 'That SCM he's hijacked is big and needs somewhere suitable to come down. And you two need to be careful where *you* land – if you look like you're dropping down somewhere dangerous, steer away quickly.'

'And watch out for overhead cables and other dangerous obstacles,' Doubleday added.

'Sir! He's about to attack again. He's hovering somewhere above us.'

'OK! Time to go!'

Hudson couldn't ever remember being more scared than at this moment. Who wouldn't be . . . jumping out of a helicopter in a storm . . . not knowing where you were going to end up . . . your worst nightmare flying above your head . . .

Without another word he edged up to the open door. The wind howled in and raindrops splattered on to the chest of his zip-up waterproof suit. He took a deep breath, forced a smile towards Molly's shocked expression and counted to three.

'OK, MOLL! SEE YOU ON THE GROUND . . . GO FOR IT!' and he jumped out.

After what seemed like an eternity, the parachute opened and Hudson felt as if he was going upwards at terrific speed. He knew he would experience this upward feeling – he'd seen parachutists on the TV. His stomach felt as if it was left behind and he gritted his teeth and bit his lip, 'WHOAHHHH . . .'

And then, much to his relief, he steadied and started to drop.

But the storm that had arrived with his enemy still raged and black clouds swirled around him. The rain washed over him in torrents and occasional dramatic bolts of forked lightning reminded him that his enemy was still close – but at least the enveloping clouds hid him from view.

Down, down, Hudson dropped, his chute rocking wildly from side to side. And then, beneath his feet the clouds thinned so that he saw a mass of buildings – a city centre – and directly below him the impressive spire of a tall church steeple rapidly reaching out towards his feet. A lightning conductor on top of the spire lit up with dramatic effect as the storm sent down yet another bolt of lightning.

This was not a good place to land.

Hudson pulled frantically on his parachute cords to change direction. Without too much difficulty, he steered away from the church steeple and headed out across the city centre and on towards the surrounding countryside. All the time the clouds thinned until small patches of blue showed up above.

He swivelled his head and glimpsed another parachute away in the distance – almost certainly Molly! He waved his arms frantically, but he knew deep down that he was too far away to be seen. And then he heard a droning sound and saw what looked like a small aircraft descending somewhere over on his left.

Hudson suddenly felt a real urge to get down on the ground.

He dropped further and saw a long straight road below – it was bordered by a thick wood on one side and open fields on the other. Pulling again on the cords, he steered over the grassy expanse and made his final descent.

A few minutes later a herd of bewildered cattle stampeded away as Hudson came in behind them. His legs easily absorbed the impact as he hit the ground and continued to run for a short distance until he ground to a halt.

He folded up the chute as quickly as possible and carried it over to the edge of the field. The rain had stopped and the sun made a welcome appearance. He took off his lightweight suit and hid it under the hedge with the folded up parachute.

Finally, he walked along the hedgerow until he found a gap wide enough to push through. He stepped out on to the long straight road and looked in both directions – no one to be seen – no cars – nothing! He looked up to the sky to see if there was any sign of the other parachute. But it was empty – no planes, no helicopters, no Molly – and thankfully, no sign of Mokee Joe!

But Hudson suddenly felt very alone.

It was the first time he could ever remember having no one to support him. GA was gone, his real parents were dead and he didn't know what had become of Mr and Mrs Brown. And now, Molly, his one true friend, had disappeared with the ever-faithful Striker. Even the men in black were temporarily out of the picture.

Hudson sat down on the edge of the road and put his head in his hands. Where *were* Molly and Striker? How could he possibly find them? What to do next? Which way to go? He was just on the verge of making a decision when a man on a bicycle appeared down the road. Hudson watched and waited patiently.

As the man finally drew alongside, Hudson saw that he was bald and had studs in both ears and rings piercing both eyebrows. Judging by the wrinkled face, he was obviously very old.

Hudson stood up to greet him. 'Excuse me . . . do you know the way to Danvers Green?'

The old man wobbled to a halt and leaned on the drop handlebars. He breathed heavily as he spoke. 'I do, son, but you're a good way off. It must be at least half an hour away . . . and that's on the community bus.'

The old man took a grubby handkerchief from the pocket of his jeans and wiped it over his glistening head. 'There's a village just up the road and you can maybe get a bus from there. What are you doing out here on your own?'

'Oh, it's a long story,' Hudson replied putting his rucksack back on to his shoulders. 'Can I beg a lift on the back of your bike?'

'I'd love to oblige, son, but I've all on managing myself. You'll just have to walk to Axelby – that's the next village. You'll be there in ten minutes if you get a move on.'

Hudson knew all about Axelby. It reassured him to know he was so close to home. 'It's OK. I'll pedal and you can ride on the back. It'll give you a rest,' he said in a matter-of-fact way.

'Well you've got spirit, son . . . I'll give you that. But I've a heavy old carcass on me these days and I doubt you'd manage it. You can give it a go if you like, though.'

The man eased back on to the seat and offered the handlebars to Hudson. He smiled sympathetically as Hudson put his leg over the crossbar and placed one foot on the raised pedal.

'Go on then, sonny. Give it a go,' the old man laughed as he suddenly produced a baseball cap and placed it on his head.

Hudson thrust the pedal down to the ground and started the bike off. It lurched forward so quickly that the old man almost fell backwards off the seat. 'WHAT THE . . .?' He grabbed Hudson's sides and clung on as the bike rapidly accelerated.

Within thirty seconds they'd reached thirty miles per hour and Hudson was still going hell for leather.

'I DON'T BELIEVE THIS IS HAPPENING!' the old man shouted into the wind. 'I MUST BE DREAMING . . . THEY'LL NEVER BELIEVE THIS AT THE SOCIAL!'

Before Hudson could really get his head down, they'd already reached Axelby and he slowed down as a shop came into view.

'That's right, son. You can drop me here if you don't mind – much as I don't really want to get off. It's the best thing that's happened to me for as long as I can remember. What's your name, boy? Where are you from?'

But Hudson didn't want to say . . . there was no time to start telling his life story . . . his priorities were to get to Danvers Green and back with Molly and Striker and whoever else might be waiting for them. 'Sorry,' was all Hudson replied. 'I've got to meet up with someone and I'm already late. If you don't mind I'll dash over to that shop and find the time of the next bus to Danvers Green.'

The man removed his cap, pushed it in his pocket and stroked his head. 'You're a strange 'un, son. But you seem to have a good heart. I'll say goodbye then. If you're going into the CCS, give my regards to Mrs Frobisher. She'll help you sort the bus times out – she's fussy but she's a good old lass. All the best, son.' And saying this, the old man climbed back on the seat of the old bike and pedalled off just as slow as before. As he disappeared around the corner, Hudson saw him take one final look back over his shoulder and scratch the back of his head.

A sign over the shop window saying 'Community Convenience Store' told Hudson what CCS stood for. As he walked through the door, an electronic beep caused him to start a little. A few seconds later, a little old woman appeared behind the counter. She wore spectacles and the lenses were so thick that it was difficult to see her eyes – they looked strange and enlarged. She was also wearing some sort of tracksuit and a baseball cap. 'And what can I be doing for you, young man?' she asked without smiling.

'Can you tell me when the next bus is due? I want to get to Danvers Green.'

'Well you'll have a long wait. There isn't another today. The next Community Bus is nine o'clock tomorrow morning. In any case, there's something odd going on up there. I've heard a rumour that folk are being evacuated . . . some sort of emergency.'

Hudson's heart skipped a beat. 'Do you know what's wrong?'

'No, but I'll soon find out. I know lots of folk around here. It's only a matter of time before . . .'

The woman stopped speaking and looked anxiously over Hudson's shoulder as something akin to a miniature jet aircraft sounded from outside. Hudson swivelled round, half-expecting to see Mokee Joe making a landing, but instead watched as an impressive motorcycle drew up in front of the shop window. As the amazing machine ground to a halt, the roar of its single jet engine quietened and was replaced by a powerful hissing sound. Like the government limousine, it had no wheels – it hovered about half a metre off the ground on a cushion of air.

The driver turned to face the window as his passenger climbed off and loosened the straps of his black, streamlined helmet. Both bikers were wearing leather jackets. The man getting off (if it was a man) was wearing scruffy denim jeans with holes in both knees and an even scruffier pair of trainers. As he turned and said something to the driver Hudson gasped at the grinning skull daubed on the back of his leather jacket.

'Oh my God! Not them again!' the old woman croaked.

'What's wrong? Who are they?' Hudson asked, sensing the woman's fear.

'I don't know their names, but they've been in here before . . . robbed me of my takings about three months ago. They're a nasty pair . . . keep out of the way, son.'

Hudson watched as the bike's passenger slammed through the door so hard that the electronic beeper shrieked and then fizzled to a comical whine.

'OK, old woman! You know why we're here. Put the money in this and give me your zapper.' He threw a blue cloth bag towards the counter and at the same time pushed Hudson rudely to one side.

The old woman sighed. 'You got away with it once, but I'll be blowed if I'm giving up my takings a second time,' she said defiantly.

The man stretched out an arm and casually swept an entire row of tin cans from a nearby shelf on to the floor. The clatter was deafening and the old woman put her hands to her ears and started shaking. She removed her metal wristband and placed it on the counter.

Hudson looked up at the face shielded by the tinted visor of the motorbike helmet. He couldn't make out the features behind it, but he could read the mind – the mind of a bully – someone who enjoyed frightening people – someone who took pleasure in spreading terror and evil – *someone like Mokee Joe!*

Hudson rarely lost his temper, but this untimely intrusion

irritated and annoyed him at the same time. He had enough on his mind already – he really needed to get to Danvers Green and nothing was going to get in his way. 'If I were you I'd get out of here before you get hurt,' Hudson said quietly and calmly to the big man in front of him.

At first, the raider had his back towards Hudson, so that the hideous skull on his jacket seemed to be mocking him. As the biker swivelled round and faced him, he laughed out loud. Without a word, he raised a hand and took a swipe straight at Hudson's head.

What happened next, the old woman would remember in vivid detail until the day she died!

changes

It all happened in a split second!

As the biker's hand swiped down towards his head, Hudson stopped it, caught hold of the wrist, and with a sickening crack, snapped it like a twig.

The biker screamed in agony and dropped to his knees.

Hudson showed little sympathy and shoved him backwards causing him to crash into the shelf from which he'd earlier swept the row of cans. But this time, the entire contents rained down so that the man suddenly found himself drowning in a sea of tinned food.

The old woman watched the dramatic scene in utter disbelief and then took the opportunity to snatch up her wristband and begin adjusting the controls.

Meanwhile, the motorcyclist outside, still sitting on his machine, heard the dreadful clatter and decided to rush in and investigate. As soon as he saw his mate writhing around on the floor and Hudson standing there, obviously in some way responsible, he drew a cosh from his jacket pocket and rushed forward to attack.

But Hudson was now in full battle mode.

At lightning speed, he threw himself forward, dropped on to his bottom and aimed the soles of his feet straight at the man's shins. Two more sickening cracks rang through the shop as the attacker's shinbones fractured cleanly. He fell forward on to his face and screamed even louder than his partner.

Hudson rolled sideways to avoid the man collapsing on to him and collided with another set of shelves, bringing down more jars and cans, most of them landing on the second shocked biker.

The old woman yelled into her 'zapper' and a moment later shouted to Hudson that the police would be arriving any minute. But Hudson didn't intend hanging around. He dashed outside and climbed on to the hovering motorcycle, the controls still set ready for the intended quick getaway. He twisted the enormous grips on the handlebars, flicked switches and studied the reaction of the dials. Within seconds he'd worked out the machine's functions and controls.

The jet engine roared – the machine raised itself up another half metre – and he was ready to go.

With the two bikers still writhing around helplessly on the shop floor, the old woman rushed to the door just in time to see the motorcycle tip backwards and rear up like an angry lion. As the machine accelerated away into the distance, she screamed her thanks, but Hudson never heard . . . he was gone, speeding along the long straight road, heading in the direction of Danvers Green.

Cruising at one hundred and twenty miles per hour, Hudson just managed to see the small dog up ahead, jumping up and down excitedly on the edge of the road. He slowed down and pulled in and his heart leapt with joy – it was Striker!

A dense wood still lined the left-hand side of the road, and Striker headed off towards it. He kept looking back, as if he wanted Hudson to follow.

'What is it, boy? Are you trying to take me to Molly? Do you know where she is?'

Striker barked enthusiastically and Hudson secured the motorcycle and ran after him. Within minutes Hudson was picking his way through the darkest wood he had ever set foot in. It was like night-time . . . dark, spooky and deathly quiet.

Striker sniffed the ground and led Hudson on – over tree roots, through dense brambles and over some strange mounds – the trees all the time closing in and cutting out the light.

'HUDSON! IS THAT YOU? I'M OVER HERE!'

Hudson had never heard such welcome words. *It was Molly.* But where was she? Striker ran over to a tree, cocked his leg up against it and then barked loudly.

'Good boy,' Hudson said to the little dog, stroking him affectionately. 'But where is she?'

'UP HERE, YOU CLOWN! WHERE DO YOU THINK I AM? FOR HEAVEN'S SAKE, GET ME DOWN!'

Hudson looked up and could hardly believe his eyes. There, in the top of the tallest of trees was Molly, caught up in a tangle of parachute material and strings.

But it was only Molly's dignity that was hurt and once Hudson saw that she was still in one piece, he had great difficulty in stopping himself from laughing. Molly snapped at him as he climbed up to free her.

'It's one thing having to parachute out of a helicopter in a storm, but to have to hang about up here like a trussed-up chicken . . . well it's just not on. What kept you, Hudson? I hope you're not laughing, 'cos it really is not funny!'

'Never mind. I'm here now. You can thank Striker for that.'

Molly calmed down. 'I know. If it wasn't for him I might have been stuck here for ever.'

That was a frightening thought and Hudson said nothing. He set about freeing her and had difficulty in stopping himself from hugging her – it felt so good to be back together again.

Striker suddenly started growling from the foot of the tree.

'OK, boy! Be patient. We'll soon be down.'

'Hudson – I know that growl,' Molly said with a sudden urgency in her voice.

Striker growled louder, and then started barking.

Hudson frantically felt in his jeans pocket and took out the small rectangular package. He removed the knife and used it to cut the strings and help Molly down. They left the parachute stuck up in the branches and quickly lowered themselves to the ground.

Striker looked anxiously at Hudson and Molly and then turned and faced deeper into the wood. As they followed the little dog's gaze, they both saw a flash of blue . . . a distant pulse of electric glow . . . and their hearts skipped a beat simultaneously.

'It's got to be him,' Hudson said quietly. 'He's back on our trail. Why didn't I pick him up . . . too many trees or perhaps too many distractions? I haven't got the faintest headache.'

'Never mind that! Hudson, let's get out of here. Do you know where we are?'

'Yes – and I've got some cool transport. Come on.'

Hudson took a last look back into the wood and almost froze at the sight of the blue glow flashing on and off as his enemy weaved through the trees towards them. All the time the light was growing bigger and brighter.

Hudson hurriedly retraced his steps back to the edge of the wood and thankfully the motorcycle was still there, parked where he'd left it. Molly's eyes opened wide when she saw it.

'Wow . . . what is that? It looks like a mean machine, Hudson. Can you drive it?'

'Well I got it here, didn't I?'

Molly couldn't argue with that.

There was some sort of carrying box on the back of the machine. She slid the lid back and placed Striker inside. And then she climbed on herself. Hudson straggled a leg over the front of the bike and turned the ignition control. Nothing happened.

Striker began barking loudly again, as if in a panic. Molly turned to face the wood and saw why.

The blue glowing figure of Mokee Joe had emerged from the trees and was hurtling towards them.

'HUDSON! HE'S HERE! WE NEED TO GO!'

He adjusted the controls and tried again. It still wouldn't start.

As Striker barked and growled and Molly screamed at Hudson to hurry, Mokee Joe drew nearer and raised his lethal fingers. They could only watch helplessly as the vicious blue bolt leapt through the air and struck the back of the bike. Molly took the brunt of it and she screamed as an agonising pain shot up her back. She fell sideways off the seat and as she hit the ground Striker fell out of the carrying box and rolled on to his back.

Mokee Joe raised his arms in triumph and set off across the narrow verge to home in on them.

Hudson reached down and helped Molly struggle back on to the bike. He made more rapid adjustments and this time the jet engine roared to life. Molly clung desperately to Hudson's waist as the bike finally moved forward.

And then, to their horror, they heard Striker's desperate bark from behind.

'OH MY GOD! STRIKER'S STILL ON THE ROAD.'

Hudson slowed and looked behind.

Striker was racing frantically after them with Mokee Joe sprinting close behind in his sinister spider-like fashion.

Hudson slowed the bike almost to a stop and shrieked encouragement to the little dog. 'COME ON, STRIKER . . . YOU CAN DO IT!'

Striker ran like fury as the demon pursuer moved in on him. Hudson and Molly watched helplessly as the Mokee Man sent out another lightning bolt, this time striking the tarmac just in front of the terrier so that some of the charge hit his metal collar. The shock took the little dog's legs from under him and Molly screamed as Striker slid forward on his face. But the plucky Jack Russell righted himself and ran even faster towards the motorcycle.

As Striker closed the gap, Hudson moved the bike slowly forward again, but Mokee Joe was almost upon them and was about to make another attack.

'HUDSON! WE'RE NOT GOING TO MAKE IT. WE CAN'T LEAVE STRIKER AND WE CAN'T GET AWAY.'

Hudson tried desperately to think what to do.

Molly was right. They couldn't leave Striker behind. Hudson would just have to stop and face his enemy now; the final showdown would not be in Danvers Green – it would have to be here, in the road.

As Mokee Joe moved in for the kill and raised his bony fingers to deliver another lethal charge, Hudson was the first to hear the thunderous roar from somewhere overhead. Mokee Joe was so intent on Hudson that he didn't hear anything – until the bullet struck the top of his head and blew his hat off.

The big red GSU helicopter swooped down and fired again. Mokee Joe, caught completely off guard, turned and fled back into the wood.

Hudson cheered inwardly and as Molly swept Striker up into her arms, he turned the throttle and sped off up the road with the helicopter hovering above them.

He and Molly looked up and saw Doubleday waving down at them. He was kneeling by the open door with a telescopic rifle. He gestured something to them and Hudson knew exactly what he was saying, that they were only a short distance from Danvers Green and they would meet up at the agreed rendezvous – the Tennyson Centre.

Whilst the helicopter roared off up the road and disappeared, Hudson stopped the bike and checked that Molly was OK. She lifted her jumper at the back and pointed to where the bolt of lightning had struck her. Hudson cringed as he saw the burn mark. It would need immediate attention when they arrived at Danvers Green.

Striker seemed to be OK. He was placed carefully back in the bike carrier, and then, with Molly's hands firmly clinging around his waist, Hudson set off at a terrific speed, determined not to stop until they finally arrived in Danvers Green.

'THIS IS IT, MOLLY! WE'RE ALMOST HOME!' Hudson shouted into the wind.

As the bike sped on, Molly shared Hudson's adrenaline rush and shrieked with delight. Striker barked enthusiastically behind her.

They were almost there . . . this time there was no stopping them. Within minutes they would be walking into the Tennyson Centre in Danvers Green to meet their welcoming committee.

But deep down, both Hudson and Molly were extremely nervous as they wondered who would actually be there, waiting for them.

16

The Price of Progress

As Hudson continued along the long, straight road, he noticed some sort of roadblock up ahead. Slowing down and drawing closer, he saw that a red and white barrier barred the way and two policemen were standing in the middle of the road.

'Oh, oh . . . trouble,' Hudson muttered loud enough so that Molly could hear.

'Don't worry,' Molly replied calmly over his shoulder. 'Remember – they're on our side.'

As Hudson drew nearer, one of the policemen put up a hand to tell him to stop and then walked towards him. Hudson saw the astonishment in the man's expression and thought to himself that it wasn't every day that you saw an eleven-year-old boy driving a powerful, state-of-the-art motorcycle with a young girl on the back and a Jack Russell terrier in the carrier.

'So you're the source of all these goings-on, are you?' the policeman said wearing a big frown. 'Well you'd better get straight over to the Tennyson Centre. They're expecting you. Do you know the way?'

Hudson nodded and said nothing. He wasn't exactly sure of the way, but he knew it was close to his old school and in any case he wanted to have a quick look around.

The weather improved further as the motorcycle cruised deeper into Danvers Green. The sun shone down on the familiar streets, but they were strangely deserted. High above their heads a helicopter circled, but other than that, there was no traffic noise to be heard.

'This is so creepy, Hudson,' Molly said nervously. 'Where is everybody?'

'I don't know. The woman at the convenience store said something about people being evacuated. Let's keep moving . . . look . . . there's our old school.'

Hudson drew up by the familiar railings bordering the school playground. They were even rustier than before. 'Brings back memories, Moll, doesn't it?'

'Yeah . . . spooky memories! Look – there's the two railings that Mokee Joe forced apart and then you straightened them again.'

Hudson looked to where Molly was pointing and saw that two of the railings were distorted and not quite as straight as the others. A sudden chill ran down his spine.

He quickly brought his mind back to the present and

looked across the empty yard. 'Have you noticed? There are more school buildings – more classrooms – it all looks a lot bigger. It's not like a junior school any more.'

'I suppose there are more kids now,' Molly said sadly. 'But where are they? It's so weird.'

'Come on. Let's go. We'll turn up your road and head towards mine – the Tennyson Centre is bound to be somewhere near Tennyson Road.' He felt Molly's grip tighten around his waist and sensed her mounting nervousness as they headed off in the direction of Molly's house.

A few moments later they turned left into Molly's road and Hudson brought the motorcycle to a juddering halt. Molly jumped off the back and ran down the road clutching the sides of her head in disbelief. As Hudson ran after her, Striker barked frantically from the carrier. And then Hudson and Molly stood side by side in the middle of the road and looked in total dismay at the sight in front of them.

All the houses had gone.

Where the streets of terraced houses had once been, a large industrial estate now stood in their place. Factory buildings spread out in all directions. To their left, a huge food processing plant stretched down the road. To their right, a large carpet showroom stood where Molly's house had been.

Molly grabbed Hudson's arm. She began to shake and then started to cry. Hudson looked at her and didn't know what to say. He walked back to the bike, lifted Striker out of the carrier and put him on the ground. The little terrier ran over to a white sign on the edge of the road and cocked his leg up against it. Hudson saw that the sign listed the factory outlets on the estate and that the Tennyson Centre was included on the list.

'Come on, Moll. Let's find the place where we're supposed to be. At least your mum and dad should be waiting.'

Molly stopped crying and dried her eyes on her sleeve. Side by side they walked on until they reached a left turn, which twenty years ago would have been the turning into Hudson's road – Tennyson Road. But like before, all the houses had gone – there were just more factories and showrooms. Another sign across the road indicated that they were heading in the direction of the Tennyson Centre.

As Hudson approached where number 13 would have been he swallowed hard and a knot formed in his stomach. A building with a large glass window stood in its place. Inside, numerous light fitments, lampshades and other electrical appliances were arranged in an impressive display. Hudson looked up at the sign painted across the top of the showroom. 'Hey, Molly! What do you make of that?'

Molly gasped as she read the sign.

CANDLESHED LIGHTING COMPANY

She gripped tight on to Hudson's arm. 'They must have got the idea from the shed at the bottom of your garden – don't you think?'

'Yeah . . . when they demolished it! It makes you sick. In some ways I wish we'd never come back here.'

'Me too,' Molly added. 'But we had to, didn't we? We had no choice.'

'You're right. Let's get on. Look . . . that's where we're heading for.'

Hudson pointed further down the road to a large, red brick

building on the left. Two policemen were standing by an entrance to a small car park. They saw Hudson and Molly walking towards them and one of the policemen raised his arm and waved them over.

A few seconds later, Hudson and Molly, with Striker still in tow, entered through an automatic sliding glass door into the foyer of a cold and functional building. An official, looking very much like someone who would be working for Doubleday, scanned them up and down and then directed them through a polished wooden door into a large room.

A long rectangular table filled the centre of the room and all sorts of people seemed to be sitting around it, as if waiting for their appearance. Hudson looked at the sea of staring faces. Molly shrieked out, half in shock, half in delight, as an oldish man and woman rushed over to greet them.

In a little room, in one corner of the building, Molly sat on her mum's knee and talked and talked, all the time her father leaning forward and holding her hands. Meanwhile, in another small room in the opposite corner of the building, Hudson sat and stared into the hollow eyes of an old woman sitting in a wheelchair – it was Mrs Brown!

Whilst Hudson held her shrivelled hands, the nurse by her side explained that Mrs Brown had first fallen ill just over twenty years ago immediately following Hudson's disappearance – she just couldn't cope without her beloved adopted son around – and then Mr Brown's death ten years ago . . .

Tears streamed down Hudson's face as he looked from Mrs Brown's sightless eyes to the nurse. 'How did my dad die?'

'Probably the way he would have wanted to – in his garden. He was digging the vegetable plot when he suffered a heart attack. He was dead even before the ambulance reached the hospital.'

'So then Mum had no one,' Hudson said, his voice trembling with emotion.

'No, apart from a few neighbours. The final straw was when her house was pulled down a year later and she was moved into an old folk's home . . . well that really hit her hard and as you can see she's just about lost the will to live.'

'*But I'm back*,' Hudson exclaimed, frustration filling his voice. 'Why doesn't she see me?'

'Because she's only there in body . . . her spirit deserted her years ago. I'm afraid she's an empty shell . . . waiting to join her husband.'

Hudson squeezed the old woman's hands and leaned forward and kissed her creased forehead. Then, without another word, he turned and walked back into the big room . . . it was time to get on with the real business . . . there was no more time for sentiment.

'There is little time to waste,' Doubleday said in his most formal and serious voice. 'It falls upon everyone here to help the young man sitting opposite me. May I introduce you to Hudson Brown and his friend, Molly Stevens. We need to find a way to help Hudson resolve his problems and ultimately our own. If this young man's enemy triumphs, then we are indeed threatened with a crisis that could have catastrophic consequences for a huge section of the population. This may sound incredibly melodramatic, but believe me, ladies and gentlemen, what I say is absolutely true.'

Hudson looked around at all the nodding heads. Most of those in attendance looked like government officials, special police and scientists. But Molly's mum and dad had been allowed to sit in and Hudson noticed that they couldn't take their eyes off their daughter. They smiled across at her and hardly seemed to notice what Doubleday was saying – Molly was so lucky!

Doubleday resumed: 'Before we continue, I have to tell you that we shall shortly be joined by two important officials. Their knowledge will be instrumental in helping us put together a plan of action.'

A car sounded outside and everyone looked towards the door.

'I think that must be them now. Hudson and Molly, I believe that you know them already, but there is no doubt that the appearance of one of them will present a shock for you both – be warned.'

The door opened and two men walked in. They headed straight towards the table. Hudson immediately recognised Professor Stokeham, but the other smartly dressed man didn't seem familiar – not at first. Handsome, well groomed, tight curly black hair, a thin moustache, Hudson estimated him to be about thirty. As soon as the young man saw them his eyes opened wide with shock.

'I CAN'T BELIEVE IT!' he shouted, putting his hands to his mouth. 'IT REALLY IS HUDSON AND MOLLY.' His teeth flashed in a wide smile as he ran towards them.

And then it was Hudson and Molly's turn to look shocked.

'Oh my God!' Molly yelled, grabbing Hudson's arm and shaking it violently. 'IT'S ASH!'

Doubleday stood up and introduced them. 'Ladies and gentlemen – Professor Stokeham of Oxford University and his leading assistant, Dr Ashley Swift. Dr Swift runs the Department of Astro Physics. For reasons I don't want to go into now, Dr Swift will have plenty of catching up to do with our two young friends. But right now we really do need to get on . . . I have just heard that the enemy has already arrived in Danvers Green.'

'Thank goodness you had the sense to evacuate everyone this morning,' Professor Stokeham said as he took one of the few empty seats around the big table.

'So the woman in the store was right. That's why there's no one around,' Molly whispered to Hudson. As she spoke, neither she nor Hudson could take their eyes off their old friend. Ash stared back, his eyes still wide as he took his place by the side of the professor.

For the next few minutes Doubleday told his audience all that they knew about Hudson's predicament. He repeated much of what he had told Hudson and Molly in the stretch limousine and emphasised the fact that news of Mokee Joe was causing a wave of terror to sweep through the country. The media had been instructed by the government to play everything down as a series of stupid and silly hoaxes – but the public was having none of it. Too many people had seen the demonic seven-foot monster in full chase, lightning charges firing from his fingers . . . Mokee Joe had caused complete chaos too many times in too many places. As far as the public was concerned – *nowhere was safe*.

'And how much does the professor know about Triotose?' Hudson asked in a loud voice.

This time, it was Professor Stokeham who answered. 'Probably more than you think, Hudson! The material came to our attention through various sources, initially via government interviews with the lady I think you refer to as the sea-witch. It all tied in with our research on the materials used in the construction of the first Alcatron spaceship – the one that your enemy used to transport himself here.'

'You mean you've found the first ship?' Hudson cried out in amazement.

Ash stood up and spoke. 'Yes, Hudson. Shortly after you and Molly vanished that night, the search began for the other ship. They guessed it was somewhere in the marsh area and it didn't take long to find it. For the last five years it's been hidden away in the old biscuit factory and I've been involved in looking after it and working on it. It didn't take long to find the ship's nuclear core.'

Doubleday took over again. 'Which brings us to our only possible solution to this hellish nightmare. We have to somehow get the creature into that ship and blast him away into space . . . back to where he came from . . . back to your planet, Hudson.'

'And you need me to pilot him there?' Hudson added in a shaky voice. 'But how can anyone possibly get him back into the ship?'

Everyone stared at Hudson.

'By luring him in,' Molly suddenly joined in. 'Hudson, they want *you* to lure him in, like an animal into a trap, and then to simply fly the both of you away. Problem solved! EXCEPT

IT'S NOT FAIR TO HUDSON!' Molly screamed around the table. 'YOU CAN'T DO THIS TO HIM – IT'S TOO DANGEROUS!'

Doubleday looked very fidgety. He glanced down at the table and scratched his chin. 'The only other alternative is to remove the Triotose from the creature so that we can destroy him, but we all know that there is only one of us here capable of doing that.'

Again, all eyes fell on Hudson.

And then, before anyone could say anything, a man in a policeman's uniform rushed in and whispered something in Doubleday's ear. Even from across the table Hudson sensed that this was something very serious. He looked across to Ash and forced a smile. Ash fidgeted in his chair and smiled nervously back – the same nervous smile that Hudson had seen so many times all those years ago.

'Well, ladies and gentlemen . . .' Doubleday rose to his feet and spread his hands on the table in front of him, '. . . it seems there has been a development.'

A whisper of worried anticipation sounded around the table.

'The Mokee Man has just taken up a position in a field near here, over in the old marsh area. Apparently he's lurking around an electricity substation.'

'Still charging up, no doubt!' the professor muttered loudly enough for everyone to hear.

Doubleday continued, 'It's true – the creature has learned to utilise electrical energy with deadly effect. But I'm afraid it's even more serious than that, Professor. It seems that Mokee Joe has communicated a message to us by infiltrating our top secret government computer network.'

Ash stood up, beads of sweat forming on his tanned forehead. 'And are we allowed to know what it says, Sir?'

'Oh yes,' the speaker said without looking at him. He continued to stare across at Hudson as he spoke. 'Basically, if Hudson Brown doesn't present himself before the creature in the next hour, then the monster will blow himself up and take most of the North Midlands with him.'

'Oh my God,' Molly gasped. 'I feel sick, Hudson. We always knew it might come to this.'

Molly's father was the next to shout up. 'And what will this Mokee Joe do should you go along with his request and present Hudson before him?'

'Oh, that has been made quite clear, Mr Stevens . . . *Hudson will be destroyed immediately . . . there and then . . . eliminated before our very eyes.*'

17

Battleground

Hudson climbed into the back of the impressive black Daimler. Molly got in beside him, Striker cradled in her arms – someone had offered to look after him, but Molly had insisted that Striker should stay with her.

Just before the car set off the door opened and Ash got in beside them. Finally, Doubleday got into the front seat beside the driver and they were on their way, Molly's mum and dad following behind, part of a small convoy of vehicles carrying police and government officials.

'You always were bright, Ash, but I never thought you would become a leading scientist. I'm impressed,' Hudson said quietly to the man by his side.

'Me too,' Molly added. 'How did you do it?'

The car cruised on towards the far side of the town, the sun disappearing behind threatening clouds. Raindrops splashed on the windscreen.

'After you and Molly left that night, following the Halloween disco, I was heartbroken. I just about had a breakdown.'

Hudson looked up at Ash's sparkling eyes. He began to feel very guilty. 'I'm so sorry, Ash. We intended Molly only to be away for a day or so . . . it was all to do with time travel and stuff like that . . .'

'Don't worry . . . I know you never meant to hurt me. Anyway, the longer you and Molly were gone, the more I kept myself busy with studying and I found that I became quite good at it – especially science and maths.'

'It doesn't surprise us, Ash,' Molly said, fluffing up Striker's ears as she spoke. 'You always did have a good brain. Remember how you used to solve those puzzles for us?'

'Yes . . . well . . . I reckoned that one day, if I studied hard enough, I might just be able to work out how to get you back. I know now it was a silly childhood fantasy, but then, if you look at the way things are turning out . . .'

'Nothing's impossible,' Hudson said. 'I think we've all seen that.'

The car's windscreen wipers swished in a steady rhythm as Ash continued. 'Well, I managed to win a place at Oxford and got heavily into astrophysics and that's when I met Professor Stokeham. He's like a god in scientific circles – a real genius.'

'Almost as clever as Hudson,' Molly quipped.

'Not quite,' Ash smiled. 'I heard all about that business in the lecture theatre. You've just about solved Stokeham's equation to show that time can loop back on itself. We always knew it was possible.'

'It had to be possible,' Hudson said modestly. 'It was GA's thinking behind taking Molly to Alcatron 3 – to return her on a time loop – so that she wouldn't be missed. Maybe what we need is a time loop to take us back twenty years . . .'

The rain hammered on to the windscreen and the driver turned the wipers up to a faster speed.

'Have you noticed, Hudson?' Molly asked, staring out of the window into the gloom. 'Whenever Mokee Joe arrives, the bad weather seems to arrive with him.'

'It's no coincidence,' Ash said. 'It's all to do with air pressure and the Earth's magnetic field. Electricity, magnetism and air pressure are all connected. The bad weather he brings with him is very localised and due to the effect of his energy field on the surrounding atmosphere.'

Molly nodded, but truthfully she didn't understand a word of it.

The car pulled up in a lane behind a string of army vehicles. A military man in full uniform ran up and opened the front passenger door.

'Well this is it, Hudson,' Ash said, putting a hand on his shoulder. 'Whatever happens you can rest assured I'll be right behind you.'

Molly gave Hudson a knowing smile. 'Just like in the old days, Ash. You were always right *behind* us then.'

Ash grinned. 'One last thing, Hudson. Before you get out, take this – you never know – it might bring you luck.'

Ash reached in his jacket pocket, took out a small object and placed it firmly in Hudson's hand. When Hudson looked down at it a large lump formed in his throat. 'Oh wow! Thanks, Ash.'

A few minutes later Hudson was led through a crowd of officials to a clearing by a farm gate higher up the lane. The gate was closed and guarded by police.

Hudson and his entourage were allowed to pass through. They walked on a few metres, stopped and looked across the marshy ground, taking in the scene.

Over towards the right-hand corner of the enclosed field, an electricity pylon stood by the side of a small, brick-built substation. The substation hummed and the pylon wires hissed as the rain began to fall incessantly. The setting looked vaguely familiar to Hudson.

And then he suddenly remembered the nightmarish out-of-body experience he'd had one night when he'd finished up lying by the side of Mokee Joe underneath a pylon in a field – perhaps this was the same place – maybe once a regular charging-up area for his enemy.

An official put up a large brolly and held it over Hudson's head. Molly, Ash, and Doubleday stood under more brollies by his side. Now the rain came down in sheets.

'He was last spotted hiding in that substation,' Doubleday said, pointing over to the corner of the field. 'Now remember – your objective is to get the Triotose – get it away from him – then we can take care of the rest.'

'Easier said than done!' Molly grumbled.

'Can't someone turn the power off?' Hudson asked, sounding somewhat agitated.

'It should be done any time now,' Doubleday answered. 'It's been difficult. We had to wait until the area was fully evacuated.'

Without another word Hudson pushed the official's brolly away and moved forward.

'Hudson! What are you doing?' Ash shouted at him as he continued to walk on.

Hudson didn't reply. He put his hands to the side of his head and walked towards the corner of the field.

'He's getting messages,' Molly said as she followed her best friend's progress. 'He's probably reading Mokee Joe loud and clear.'

She was right.

Hudson stopped a few metres from the substation. There was still no sign of Mokee Joe, but the words were forming clearly in his head:

We meet for the final time, Tor-3-ergon. My purpose is about to be fulfilled. You have no choice. Either I destroy you now and return to the Plexus System in the rescued ship . . . or I destroy us all. The explosion will be catastrophic for much of this domain.

Hudson took a few more cautious steps and scanned around, desperate to spot his enemy. At the same time, the crackling in the overhead cables suddenly stopped . . . fizzled out . . . the substation stopped humming. The power supply was cut!

And then Mokee Joe rushed out from the substation and planted himself directly under the pylon. At the same time, more words flooded into Hudson's head: *The fools have switched off the power supply. But it is too late. I have acquired more than enough energy to trigger the Triotose reaction.*

Hudson moved towards his enemy and felt a wave of revulsion as he took in Mokee Joe's close up appearance.

The evil alien face with its staring black eyes mocked him . . . grinning and scowling at the same time. The mouth was open showing its drooling fangs, as if ready to bite, and the cracked skin around the entire face looked discoloured and pockmarked – like diseased flesh.

But the strangest thing of all was that there was no glow – no crackling blue charge – as if, like the pylon, Mokee Joe's energy supply was switched off.

Now was the time to strike.

Hudson clenched his fists so hard that his fingernails dug into his tough skin and drew blood. *OK, Mokee Joe . . . this is it*, he thought to himself. *Let's see what you're really made of!*

18

Secret Weapons

Hudson tensed his neck muscles, lowered his head and charged at Mokee Joe like a raging bull. He decided that speed combined with brute strength might just be enough to take his enemy by surprise and flatten him to the ground.

But as Hudson reached his enemy and braced himself for the collision, nothing happened – he just kept on running – straight through him!

Turning back he stared in disbelief at the mocking figure. Over in the distance a similarly shocked audience of onlookers shouted towards him.

'HUDSON . . . WHAT ARE YOU PLAYING AT?' he heard Molly yelling at the top of her voice.

As Hudson realised what had happened, he cursed himself

under his breath: '*Idiot! They can't see him because he's not there . . . it's not the real Mokee Joe . . . it's a thought projection . . . and I fell for it!*'

He walked back to the centre of the pylon and waved his hand back and forth through the virtual image as another distant yell confirmed his theory. 'WATCH OUT, SON . . . HE'S ABOVE YOU!'

Hudson looked up, but it was too late.

The real seven-foot demon dropped like a stone from his hidden perch up on the pylon. Hudson's blood froze as two huge boots thudded down only inches away from his own and suddenly the evil figure was towering over him – glowing like never before – deep blue, flowing into purplish red, and hissing and crackling like a thousand fireworks.

Before Hudson had chance to react, Mokee Joe grabbed him in a bear hug and unleashed a huge electrical charge into his body. Hudson screamed as the searing pain racked through his body from head to toe. As the bony hands released him, he reeled backwards and fell heavily to the ground, his brain struggling to stay conscious. Somewhere in his dizziness he heard Mokee Joe shriek out in high-pitched electronic glee.

However, Hudson was strong and his body quickly recovered. He stirred and dragged himself up on to his elbows, but to his horror Mokee Joe moved more quickly and descended like a huge vampire bat over his prostrate body.

Just as before, during the attack on Candleshed, Hudson found himself with Mokee Joe kneeling astride him, pinning him to the ground, the pincer-like hands closing in around his neck. He tried desperately to grab the tightening fingers and pull them away, but the Mokee Man simply shot more electricity into his body and continued to squeeze the life out of him.

The rain splattered on Hudson's face and his eyes began to glaze over.

Mokee Joe's face moved closer, the tight black lips grinning at his increasing predicament. All Hudson could do was to stare back into those black, alien eyes and read the real evil there – how his father must have hated him to create such a monster.

Hudson tensed his throat muscles, but Mokee Joe's hands only squeezed tighter and everything started to go blurry. As his lungs became increasingly starved of oxygen, he felt the life beginning to drain from his body – it seemed there was nothing he could do.

This is it . . . Hudson thought to himself. *It's really over this time . . . I've lost . . . it's all been for nothing.*

Mokee Joe squeezed ever so slightly tighter, and even in Hudson's dying moments he could sense that his enemy was savouring the act of killing him. Fleeting images flashed through Hudson's mind – images of all those he'd loved in his brief life – GA, Mr and Mrs Brown and, of course, Molly and Ash.

Ash!

Hudson suddenly remembered the wave of emotion that had washed over him when Ash had presented him with that very special object in the car. How could he have forgotten about it at a time like this – it had saved him once before and it might just save him again. As he struggled to reach into his jeans pocket, Mokee Joe leaned forward so close that Hudson could smell his foul oily breath. At the same time a final message formed in his aching head:

As you know well, Tor-3-ergon, your father designed me to make me hungry for your death, but I have learnt to think for myself. The Triotose is stored safely in the heart of my circuitry – though I never had any intention of detonating it – I value my own existence too much! Since my arrival on this planet I have enjoyed inflicting terror on young humans and my enjoyment will only increase with time – but for now I will gain more satisfaction than you can ever imagine by terminating your existence.

Farewell, Tor-3-ergon.

As Mokee Joe prepared to crush Hudson's neck to pulp and simultaneously fire a lethal charge of high-powered electricity into his limp body, a frenzied bark sounded from somewhere behind Hudson's head.

Mokee Joe glanced up as Striker rushed towards him.

Without hesitation the little dog jumped straight over Hudson's body and sank his teeth savagely into one of Mokee Joe's arms. But the fiend didn't even flinch. He released his grip from Hudson's throat and shook his arm so violently that Striker let go and rolled on to his back. Not content with this, Mokee Joe then picked the terrier up by the collar and hurled him towards one of the great iron pylon legs. Hudson vaguely heard Molly's distant screams as the little dog's body struck the metal upright and fell stunned to the ground. And then Striker lay quite still.

Hudson, his throat momentarily freed, managed to gasp a little more oxygen – Striker had provided a distraction and now was the time to take full advantage of it.

As Mokee Joe's hands went back to his throat, Hudson brought out from his sodden trouser pocket the clear resin block containing the carcass of his long lost spider friend. Ash had held on to Spiffy and saved him for all those years – it was a memento from a true and loyal friend – and now it was going to prove useful again.

Hudson mustered all his remaining strength and thrust the curved surface of the block towards his enemy's grotesque nose.

Mokee Joe's expression changed dramatically as Hudson rammed the encased spider with incredible force into his cracked synthetic flesh so that it embedded itself firmly into his face. He reeled backwards, let go of Hudson and tried desperately to remove it. But the block was well and truly stuck – like a pebble set in concrete.

As Mokee Joe fell away from his chest, Hudson raised himself back on to his elbows and watched in awe as his enemy's eyes rolled inwards, desperately trying to see what was planted on the bridge of his nose. And as he finally made out the perfectly preserved arachnid at such close up quarters, his reaction was dramatic. He keeled over and fell on to his back, clutching at his face and screaming an electronic, panic-filled scream.

The crowd cheered from behind as they watched the tables turn in Hudson's favour.

Now it was his turn to tower over his enemy.

As the rain continued to come down in torrents, Hudson noticed the lines of crackling blue electricity shooting out from the Mokee Man's body into the surrounding damp grass. And then he noticed the small pools of water collecting around them.

Of course, he thought to himself, *this is the old marsh . . . puddles would form here quicker than anywhere else*.

With Mokee Joe writhing around on the ground, still clutching at the dead spider and still failing to remove it, Hudson's brain worked at lightning speed. He began to press down on Mokee Joe's body.

Suddenly, Mokee Joe's desperate fingers succeeded in removing the resin block. He plucked it out of his face and cast it far into the distance – now, angrier than ever, he turned his attention back to the small boy sitting astride his chest.

Hudson saw the mixture of hatred, annoyance and curiosity in his enemy's expression. He couldn't work out why Hudson was pressing down on him – perhaps Tor-3-ergon had finally flipped.

But Hudson knew exactly what he was doing.

As Mokee Joe reached out for his neck, Hudson pushed even harder and then brought out his second secret weapon.

Tight in the other pocket of his jeans was his valued gift from Bikram – the long knife! Hudson drew it out and still kneeling over his enemy he managed to slash open Mokee Joe's coat. Whilst the monster writhed and wrestled with him, Hudson slit open the ragged shirt to reveal a complex of wires and circuitry. Finally he saw what he was looking for – a small rectangular block of shiny metal resting amongst the tangle of circuits. The *Triotose*, just as Mokee Joe had said, concealed within his heart.

As Mokee Joe screamed another chilling high-pitched scream, his circuitry hissed and crackled and his surrounding blue glow burned brighter than ever as he concentrated all his remaining energy into one final surge of electrical charge, ready to fire into Hudson's body.

But Hudson had already grabbed the block. He pulled it free and threw it back towards the onlookers. 'GET THIS AND TAKE IT AWAY!' he screamed.

'OK! GET OUT OF THE WAY AND LEAVE HIM TO US!' Doubleday's voice shouted.

Hudson glanced behind and saw several police marksmen raise their rifles. But now he was fully recovered and determined to finish the job himself. He placed both hands on Mokee Joe's torn upper body and pressed down with all his strength. No way could he stop his enemy's electronic breathing – or collapse the super-strong frame – but that wasn't the intention.

Mokee Joe sneered . . . he screamed again . . . he glowed even brighter . . . it was time to fry the boy on his chest!

And that's when an ominous pool of dark, peaty liquid seeped up and surrounded Mokee Joe's body.

It was such a simple scientific principle – as the monster's heavy body sank lower into the marshy ground, the rainwater displaced upwards into a huge puddle. Mokee Joe was now lying in a miniature lake.

Unfortunately for Mokee Joe, he hadn't read the situation, and as he unleashed his ultimate, massive charge there was an almighty blinding blue flash and a deafening bang rang out across the marshes.

The explosion was phenomenal and Hudson was thrown a huge distance through the air, landing heavily and awkwardly in a crumpled heap. Mokee Joe lay in the same place, blackened and spent. Somewhere nearby, Striker still lay unconscious.

The crowd of onlookers broke through the tape and ran towards the battlefield.

Molly was the first to kneel over Hudson's body. She screamed hysterically as she saw his eyes wide open . . . lifeless . . . staring nowhere.

'He's dead! I can't believe it. Hudson's dead!'

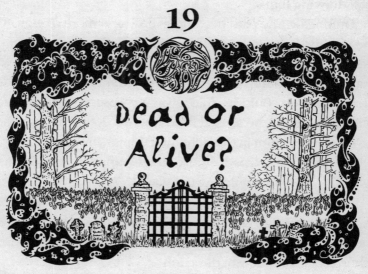

19

Dead or Alive?

Hudson looked up at Molly's horrified expression. She was sobbing like a baby. Whilst various other officials joined her and gathered round, he suddenly found himself sitting up and beginning to drift out of his body.

He really had no idea whether he was dead or alive.

Beyond the resulting panic and pandemonium, something was pulling at him from elsewhere, and right now he had to get to that something . . . the force growing stronger with every passing second.

Hudson allowed his out-of-body self to drift away from the crowd and over to the edge of the field. He passed straight through a thick hawthorn hedge and into a dark wood. The peace was blissful – the darkness, welcoming.

Though he was able to pass through trees or any other obstacles, he chose to drift along a lonely, half-overgrown pathway. Somewhere in the distance, the powerful force was still drawing him.

Drifting on, the path becoming more and more overgrown, he saw the first tombstone lying amongst long grass over on his left. A ghostly figure stood in front of it. The figure was hard to make out in detail because a bright light surrounded it, but Hudson could see that it was a corpse. It didn't frighten him in the least – he sensed it was there to help and it seemed to be pointing him in the right direction. As he moved further along the spooky path, more graves appeared with more ghostly occupants pointing the way.

Finally, the familiar spire of St Michael de Rothchilde appeared through the trees and Hudson knew exactly where he was. He had simply approached the abandoned Norman church from a different direction.

Passing through the ancient gate, Hudson saw a long line of illuminated spectral shapes standing alongside the path, all pointing towards the boarded-up, arched doorway.

Everything was so dreamlike, so unreal, and Hudson found he couldn't react . . . no emotion . . . no fear . . . just an uncontrollable desire to get to the source of the power that was drawing him.

He passed through the ancient door into the derelict church and found himself looking around the vast empty space within. He turned and faced the altar steps and saw the spot where GA had once met up with them – this seemed to be the source of the power and it drew Hudson towards it. But as he finally reached the bottom of the altar steps a coldness swept through the building inducing a feeling of emptiness and despair in his heart.

Hudson had never felt so alone.

He allowed himself to drift to the top of the altar steps. He looked with tearful eyes towards where the altar would have once stood and beyond to a vandalised stained-glass window.

He instinctively allowed his innermost thoughts to flow freely – as if he expected someone to pick up on them:

Why am I here? What's happening to me?
I don't know why I've had to go through all this . . . first, losing my mum . . . and then my dad wanting to get rid of me . . . terrorising me with a monster made by his own hands. And now I don't even know whether I'm dead or alive . . . can somebody please help me?

Hudson looked down as an eerie blast of wind hurried some long-dead leaves across the stone slabs in front of the altar space. Everything seemed so cold and empty . . . and hopeless. He lifted his 'out-of-body' eyes back towards the stained-glass window and saw the tall gothic figure of his enemy etched into one of the glass panes. His heart filled with total despair at the sight of it.

And then he saw the plaque hanging loosely from the wall. From his distant position he was still able to focus on it and read the words:

Lock the door, sweet babe, shut out the night

Keep the tallow candles burning bright
Pray and wait for God to exercise his ploy
Deliver forth the Chosen One, the Golden Boy
Only he can smite the evil from this land
Until that time beware the demon Mokee Man

(Anon 1793)

And as he finished reading the words, a warm glow began to seep through him, starting from his feet and slowly working its way up to his knees and on into his chest and arms. And then as the warmth entered his head he became aware of a brightness shining from behind. And turning around, Hudson saw that the church was filled with ghostly shining figures, like the ones he'd seen outside.

He knew at once that the spectral congregation was made up of the dead from the graveyard. During their time on Earth, they too had endured the terrifying ordeal of Mokee Joe. He had lived amongst them for the last two hundred years and now they had come to see the 'Golden Boy' who had tried so hard to destroy him . . . to smite the evil from their land and bring peace to the old Borough of Danvers Green.

As Hudson stared in awe at his phantom audience he became aware that they were all looking past him towards the altar space. He quickly turned back to see a golden sphere of light resting on the stone slabs about three metres away. He watched, fascinated, as the orb grew in size until its curved surface reached out and almost touched his nose. At the same time, the warm glow in his body grew more intense. The orb flattened and Hudson experienced a wave of joy as GA's smiling face appeared inside the golden circle. 'Tor-3-ergon . . . we meet again.'

'GA!' Hudson exclaimed. 'I can't believe it. I never thought I'd see you again.'

GA's face shimmered in the glowing circle of light. 'You only think you see me. Truly we are experiencing each other's infinite existence at a given point in time and space.'

Hudson wasn't sure he understood, but it didn't matter. He was overjoyed to see his Guardian Uncle again.

GA continued. 'You have done well, Tor-3-ergon. You have almost destroyed the Mokee Man.'

'Have I killed him?' Hudson asked.

'Physically, yes, but he still carries a strong element of your father's spirit and that spirit lives on.'

'I don't know what you mean,' Hudson uttered in surprise.

'Be patient . . . you will shortly learn his fate as well as your own. And remember . . . goodness is always repaid by goodness. You have nothing to fear . . .'

GA's face smiled and then slowly faded away. But the golden ring remained . . . and another face appeared. It was the face of a woman. Though it shimmered in the bright light, Hudson saw that it was embraced by long, straight, silver hair – it was the most beautiful face Hudson had ever seen.

As the image became clearer, the eyes stared at him and Hudson read the expression – a mixture of love and curiosity.

He knew immediately that it was the face of his mother – Joetan-3-ergon.

Dear child, the words filled his mind. *I have never had the chance to show you my love – and yet I have never stopped loving you. You are with me constantly.*

Hudson was speechless. He looked into the kind eyes and yearned to reach out and show his affection.

Don't trouble your heart, Tor-3-ergon . . . I understand your feelings. For now you only need know that we are not entirely lost to each other. Go back and lead the life that fate has thrust upon you. All will be well . . .

The eyes filled with tears and Hudson felt his heart simultaneously fill with love for the mother he had never had . . . and then, like before, the vision faded.

Though the ring of gold still remained, the surrounding atmosphere suddenly changed.

Hudson felt a chill. He turned and saw that the congregation had faded away.

Hudson sensed that something sinister was taking place.

He turned back and saw that a small black spot had formed at the centre of the golden circle.

The tiny inner-circle of darkness expanded, the blackness spreading outwards, blotting out more and more of the brighter larger circle. Now, the entire ring was black apart from a thin ring of brightness around its edge.

And that's when a very different face appeared, a dull, mournful face, its grey complexion making it stand out from the blackness. It was a face full of torment.

Hudson gawped in horror.

As soon as he saw the four distinct lobes on the enlarged head he knew who he was looking at.

It was his father . . . Dek-3-ergon.

The expression on the twisted face was full of hatred and Hudson felt himself recoil under the terrifying intensity of the stare. He recognised the same look of hatred he had seen so many times on the face of Mokee Joe.

'Why do you hate me so much, Father?' Hudson cried. 'I never meant to hurt you . . . I just wanted to be your son . . . to love you . . . as I would have loved my mother.'

The face screamed back at him, 'BUT IT WAS YOU WHO KILLED HER . . . YOU KILLED JOE . . . MY WIFE . . . THE ONLY PERSON WHO EVER LOVED ME!'

'But how could I have known that she would die giving birth to me? I would have loved her like you did. I *still* love my mum.'

There was a pause – a pronounced silence as the words seemed to strike home – the face changed.

Hudson saw compassion in his father's eyes. He sensed his father's genuine remorse as some small part of him began to reach out with love and forgiveness.

'I regret that you are right, my son,' the face said in a mournful tone. 'I have been unjust and now I am trapped in a void of sorrow and frustration, doomed to stay here for eternity. I can only try to make amends.'

'How?' Hudson asked.

By removing that which I created to destroy you.'

'Mokee Joe?'

'Yes! You may have destroyed his physical body, but the creature has taken on a large part of my mental state and developed it into a spiritual entity as evil and misguided as my own. This ancient place of worship lies amongst massive energy fields – both physical and spiritual. Even as I speak his mental projection combines these forces and grows stronger as it comes upon you . . .'

Hudson sensed the threat contained in his father's words.

Suddenly, he felt compelled to look behind and as he turned his entire being was struck numb with terror.

There at the back of the church was Mokee Joe like he'd never seen him before.

The figure was a phantom like himself, but haggard and dishevelled, hideous in every detail and reaching upwards towards the roof of the church . . . *at least thirty feet tall* . . . a towering monstrosity of pure evil.

The gigantic Mokee Joe started to drift towards him, hands outstretched, face leering, and Hudson sensed its desire to smother him, devour him once and for all . . . eradicate him totally from any form of existence.

As the awful vision moved ever closer, the circle in front began to grow larger. The face of his tormented father shimmered and the mouth moaned its final words.

'Forgive me, Tor-3-ergon . . . please find it in your heart to forgive me . . .'

And then Hudson felt revulsion as his father's mouth grew out of all proportion to the rest of his contorted grey face. The mouth became huge, black and cavernous and some sort of wind seemed to draw things towards it. Hudson felt himself being sucked towards the growing black hole and it took all his will and strength to resist.

Meanwhile the towering form of his enemy loomed closer.

But as Mokee Joe's mental projection reared up and prepared to attack, it suddenly became aware of the huge black entity and immediately began to back away.

Hudson concentrated all his will and clung to his position and watched in horror as his enemy braced himself and tried in vain to stop himself from being drawn towards the enveloping circle.

But Hudson's father was stronger.

Mokee Joe's hat was the first to go. It shot off the monster's head, flew across the church and disappeared into the black void of his creator's mouth. The creature's eyes filled with panic as, one by one, the coat, trousers, boots and other hideous garments followed suit.

Hudson felt sick at the sight of his towering naked enemy.

The horrific monster had never looked so vulnerable – standing there in nothing but cracked, synthetic flesh. Trailing metal circuitry hung from his open chest where Hudson had earlier torn it apart.

And as the creature's face contorted, screaming agonising, silent screams, the wind reached its maximum force so that Mokee Joe's body began to break up into fragments – hair, eyes, ears, limbs and then the circuitry, each grotesque item swirling and disappearing for ever into the all-consuming black hole.

And finally, Mokee Joe's mental state was no more.

Hudson held on and looked back to the circle and saw that the black hole had started to decrease in size. It closed up and became a normal mouth again – his father's mouth. And then the face slowly reformed, but now it seemed to wear a more peaceful expression and finally it smiled at him.

It is done, Tor-3-ergon. Mokee Joe is no more. Close your eyes, wait a few seconds and then open them again . . .

Hudson smiled back, desperately wanting to show his father the forgiveness that he knew he yearned for. But he did as he was told and closed his eyes, and before he could open them again he felt something wet on his cheek. He took a deep breath, opened his eyes and saw Molly staring down at him. Striker was by his side licking at his face.

'He has a faint pulse,' one of the officials was saying as he pressed on the side of his neck.

'Hudson . . . honestly . . . we thought you were dead,' Molly said softly to him.

Hudson smiled feebly back at her, still not sure what was happening. 'So did I,' he whispered. 'So did I.'

For the next few days, Hudson, Molly, Ash, Striker, Molly's parents and a whole host of government scientists and officials took up residence in the old biscuit factory. Hudson's eyes marvelled at the transformation that had taken place there.

The golden vats, copper tanks and lines of silver pipes had all long since been removed. The huge factory spaces, which had once housed them, had now been converted into plush suites of scientific laboratories and offices.

But the most amazing conversion of all was that of the old flour room.

Hudson remembered clearly the afternoon of the school trip, when he'd seen his enemy reclining in sinister fashion on top of the flour stacks. But now the room only housed one item – a spaceship!

It was the ship that Mokee Joe had arrived in all those hundreds of years ago.

Ash had led a team of scientists in searching for the ship and also in its subsequent recovery from below the marsh. He and his team had been working on its function ever since.

Now, with Hudson's brain on the case, Professor Stokeham had suggested a possible final solution to resolve Hudson and Molly's strange predicament and everyone was very excited about it.

Hudson sat up night after night with Professor Stokeham, Ash and other eminent scientists poring over calculations. Molly waited patiently in the background, talking endlessly to her parents and occasionally visiting Mrs Brown – the old lady barely recognised her and continued to stare lifelessly into space. Striker mooched around, somehow sensing that his future was in the balance.

Exactly six days after their arrival in Danvers Green, Hudson and the professor made the breakthrough that they had all waited for. The calculations were complete.

The following night, the ship was transported to a secret clearing close to the old church and preparations made for lift-off.

Just as before, following the Halloween disco, Hudson climbed aboard with Molly by his side – but this time there was no GA to lead them. Mokee Joe's physical body, charred and blackened, had been zipped up in a black rubber body bag and it was stowed on board – the sight of it still made Hudson cringe.

Just before take off, Hudson and Molly said farewell to their small army of helpers. Molly kissed her parents and Hudson shook Ash's hand so hard that he inadvertently caused Ash to wince.

'See you soon, Ash . . . I hope,' Hudson smiled up at him.

'Take care. I'll keep this safe for your return,' Ash said, taking the small object from his pocket.

Hudson warmed at the sight of Spiffy, still intact in the resin block. Ash must have searched high and low for it after the battle.

He turned to the chief man in black. 'Thanks, Doubleday . . . or should I say Edward Lombard Thompson-Jones?' Hudson grinned.

'So you knew all the time!' Doubleday mused. 'I should have known.'

'Yes . . . "Doubleday" was just a play on words . . . DD or Double D . . . stands for "Doomsday", the top-secret name for the project.'

'Exactly right, Hudson! As I've often said . . . you're one very special young man!'

Finally, it was time to say goodbye to Striker. Hudson and Molly took it in turns to hold him whilst he affectionately licked each of their faces. Hudson looked into Striker's eyes and sensed that the little dog knew that they were parting ways.

'Get him back to the sea-witch, Ash. She needs him more than we do. It's where he belongs . . .'

'Don't worry. It's as good as done,' Ash said, taking Striker into his arms.

Hudson and Molly gave him a last tickle behind his ears and moved towards the ramp of the ship, hardly daring to look back.

* * *

Just before midnight, the ship raised itself slowly upwards into a perfectly clear sky. The crowd of people below marvelled at the ease with which it climbed away and disappeared amongst the stars.

It was the second time that Ash had seen his friends depart, but this time he felt no remorse. He walked away, clutching the resin block and whistling to himself.

Later that evening as Molly's parents arrived home, settled themselves down on the settee and looked with jubilation into each other's eyes, high above their heads the small spaceship moved out of the solar system and entered deep space.

Hudson pressed a series of buttons on the control panel and jettisoned the zipped-up body bag into space. He and Molly watched with satisfaction as Mokee Joe's mummified spent body twisted and reeled and drifted away to eternity. It seemed such a final ending and it gave Hudson a great peace of mind to witness it.

And then, as the ship accelerated at a fantastic rate, he and Molly saw the stars begin to merge into straight lines. Hudson made final adjustments to the automatic pilot and turned to Molly.

'Whatever happens, Moll . . . you know that . . .' He began to choke on his words.

Molly took hold of his wrists and smiled at him. 'I get your drift. You don't have to say anything, Hudson. I really wouldn't want to be anywhere else.'

The two of them hugged each other and Molly cried out in mock pain, reminding Hudson how strong he was. And then she kissed him tenderly on the cheek.

They took a final look out of the cockpit window. The ship was still accelerating and rapidly approaching the speed of light. Outside, silver rods of starlight were beginning to curve slightly. Inside the ship, Hudson and Molly began to feel strange – light and wobbly.

It was time to climb into their sleep capsules.

Moments later the ship's nuclear core kicked in and delivered an unimaginable thrust of energy, accelerating the craft beyond the speed of light. Its trajectory was still set dead straight, but time and space started to curve back on itself.

Hudson and Molly had embarked upon a fantastic journey – a voyage along the calculated co-ordinates of a time loop. And if Hudson's calculations were correct, the ship would eventually finish up slightly further back from the point in time and space from which it had started – twenty years to be precise!

Hudson slept a worried sleep in his sleep capsule.

Deep within his subconscious, he was praying for all he was worth that he and the Stokeham team of scientists had got their calculations correct.

The lone figure of a reclusive UFO spotter stood on the edge of the old marsh. Tonight his dream would come true.

He'd heard all the rumours about government officials and clearings and strange goings-on in the old marsh area. He'd searched around all night, looking for clues, constantly staring up at the heavens. And now, during the early hours of Sunday morning, a bright light appeared on the distant horizon.

The silent observer knew at once that it wasn't a plane. His equipment picked up no noise, and in any case, the light was moving too fast.

He watched in awe as the light grew bigger and moved towards him. He desperately adjusted his tripod and cameras and tried to photograph the ship as it descended somewhere in the distance. But it all happened too quickly.

He left his equipment and tried to run over towards where the ship had landed, but the two small figures had already disembarked . . . the spacecraft already concealed below the watery surface.

Some hours later, as the UFO spotter solemnly packed away his equipment and wondered if anyone would believe his story, a few miles away a young boy sat on the doorstep of a small terraced house. He stared up at the stars and looked toward the constellation of Orion. For the first time, the sight of the Hunter didn't make him feel homesick. He smiled to himself as a familiar voice sounded from over his shoulder.

'Is that you, lad?'

Hudson turned as the door of number 13 opened behind him.

Mr Brown's stern features glowered downwards. 'Whatever are you doing sitting there? And what time do you call this?'

'Sorry, Dad! The Halloween disco went on a bit longer than expected.'

'Halloween disco, indeed! Your mother's being going out of her wits with worry. For some reason she got it into her head that you were never coming back. Are you going to sit there all night, lad?'

At the mention of Mrs Brown, Hudson felt his heart leap with joy. 'Sorry, Dad.' He got up and brushed past Mr Brown into the narrow hallway. He saw that the sitting room door was slightly open and as he moved towards it, his adoptive father muttered something about discos and how they shouldn't be allowed to go on so late.

Hudson pushed open the door and saw Mrs Brown reclining in the big armchair. She snoozed and fidgeted restlessly and as Hudson drew closer he saw the tracks of her tears down each side of her face.

Pugwash was curled up on her knee, the large black cat making a strange combination of purring and snoring sounds. Hudson had to stop himself from shrieking out in delight at the sight of his pet, but then he noticed the cup of chocolate on the small table by Mrs Brown's side. It was cold and untouched.

Hudson gulped with emotion at the sight of it.

He leaned over and kissed his mum softly on the forehead. 'It's only me, Mum . . . Hudson . . . I'm home.'

Look out for Peter J Murray's
next trilogy, beginning with

Bonebreaker

A holiday with his friend's family seems like the perfect opportunity
for Billy to forget about the creepy things that
have been happening at home.

But when the sinister incidents continue and become worse, he
discovers a past history that he never knew he had,
is catching up with him...

As well as whatever is haunting him...

Read the first two parts of
Hudson's adventure in

MoKee Joe
IS COMING

MoKee Joe
RECHARGED